A Guide to B.C. Indian Myth and Legend

A Guide to B.C. Indian Myth and Legend

A Short History of Myth-Collecting and a Survey of Published Texts

by Ralph Maud

Talonbooks • Vancouver • 1982

published with assistance from the Canada Council, the British Columbia Heritage Fund and the Government of British Columbia through the British Columbia Cultural Fund and the Western Canada Lottery Foundation

Talonbooks
201 1019 East Cordova
Vancouver
British Columbia V6A 1M8
Canada

This book was typeset by Mary Schendlinger, designed by Karl Siegler and printed by Hemlock Printers for Talonbooks.

Cover design: David Robinson

First printing: November 1982

Canadian Cataloguing in Publication Data

Maud, Ralph, 1928-
  A guide to B.C. Indian myth and legend

  Includes index.
  ISBN 0-88922-189-8

  1. Indians of North America—British Columbia—Religion and Mythology—Bibliography.
  2. Indians of North America—British Columbia—Legends—Bibliography.   3. Ethnology—British Columbia—Bibliography.
  4. Ethnologists—British Columbia—Biography.
  Z1209.2.C22B754   016.97000497   C82-091321-9

Frontispiece Photo: Tralahaet, or "Gitiks," known under the English name of Frank Bolton, recorded Tsimshian songs for Marius Barbeau at Arrandale on the Nass River in 1927—"the most useful and best informed of all our singers" (Barbeau, "Tsimshian Songs," p. 100). Photo: National Museum of Man, National Museums of Canada, negative #69595.

Table of Contents

Table of Contents

List of Illustrations

Chapter I
Introduction

Of the proposed series, *The Indian History of British Columbia,*
Wilson Duff completed one volume only, *The Impact of the
White Man* (B.C. Provincial Museum 1964). Presumably a
subsequent volume would have dealt with Indian history as
seen by the Native people themselves: the creation of the
world, the flood and other disasters, the legends behind local
topography, the founding of the great families and their crests,
the doings of shamans and warriors. Attention would have
been paid to the important tales about Raven, Coyote,
Bear, Beaver, Mink, Bluejay, and all the other animals whose
adventures in the early times were just as real as later history,
so it was said. This book does not attempt such a comprehensive
treatment of the Indian world view, but presents a survey of
the materials available for doing so.

To use the present-day provincial boundary of British
Columbia as a cut-off point is not so arbitrary as it might
seem. Of course, myths and legends know no such confines;
to track any single theme would take us beyond the Pacific
area into the world at large. But since we are concerned not so
much with myths as with myth collecting, British Columbia
presents an interesting case. Franz Boas and his close associates

9

did their earliest field work here, concurrent with an indigenous strain of folklorists. The rise and fall of the National Museum's interest in the West Coast is a curious phenomenon. Lately we have had a rush of expert linguists doing a massive salvaging of the languages, which has abetted the new concern by Native leaders for all aspects of their old culture, including myths and legends. B.C. thus provides a varied panorama for what I shall call "mythography," the study of how a people's oral traditional literature becomes available to us in published form.

I want first, however, to focus on three individuals who worked just outside the perimeter of British Columbia. They are exemplary: their myth collecting is notable not only for its intrinsic quality but also for the clarification it provides on the process of transmission of myths from performance to paper. (1) Emile Petitot was an Oblate missionary in the Northwest Territories from 1862 to 1883, and in the midst of extreme privation wrote down serene ethnographic observations. His *Traditions Indiennes du Canada Nord-Ouest* (1886) is still kept in print by its Paris publisher. (2) Archie Phinney worked in the field for only one season to produce his outstanding *Nez Percé Texts* (1934); but among Franz Boas's students, Phinney was unique, a full-blooded Native of the tribe he was assigned to study. (3) In 1970, a well-respected anthropologist, Catharine McClellan, decided to throw caution to the winds and used the word "masterpiece" in relation to a Native story. In publishing *The Girl Who Married the Bear* (Ottawa 1970) she dared to add the subtitle: "A Masterpiece of Indian Oral Tradition."

Petitot and Missionary Predilections

Until the last decade there was nothing by or about Emile Petitot in English, beyond a few encyclopedia entries. When attention was recently focussed on the Mackenzie Valley, the Northern Science Research Group of the Department of Indian Affairs and Northern Development astutely apportioned some of its funds to the editing of two resplendent volumes

10

Emil Petitot, ordained priest on 15 March 1862, just before his departure for the Canadian Northwest.

entitled *The Amerindians of the Canadian North-West in the 19th Century, as seen by Emile Petitot* (1971). The samples of stories reprinted from *Traditions Indiennes du Canada Nord-Ouest* (1886, with the Native language texts as found in the 1888 edition) are strictly confined to the Mackenzie Valley Eskimo and Loucheaux, but there are enough of them to convince us that Petitot had a deft hand at taking down a specific telling of a story without losing its clarity and charm. I am persuaded as to his authenticity by one passage in particular. Not only is the teller of the story named, with date and place of telling (Fort Good Hope, December 1870—Petitot in his eighth year of residence in those parts), but the precise wording seems "right":

> . . . when day came, the evening-wife disappeared once more, but her husband followed her at a distance. "Where is she going, and why does she want to go?" he wondered. Then he saw her walking naked into a black, filthy swamp. There she stood upright, with a black snake wound around her. Witness of this abomination, *Dindjié* was thunder-struck, and left the evening-wife where she was . . . she ran into the swamps and disappeared. Nothing was ever heard of her again. When the Hudson's Bay Company came here, we thought it was the bad evening-wife who had returned to us.[1]

The business about the snake is surely something a priest

---

[1]Told by Sylvain Vitoedh to Emile Petitot, *The Amerindians of the Canadian North-West in the 19th Century, as Seen by Emile Petitot,* Vol. II: The Loucheux Indians, ed. Donat Savoie (Ottawa: Department of Indian Affairs and Northern Development 1971) pp. 133-134. Translation from the French by L.A.C.O. Hunt. Another translation, by Thelma Habgood, appears in "Indian Legends of North-Western Canada, by Emile Petitot" *Western Canadian Journal of Anthropology* 2 (1970/1) 94-129 on pp. 99-100. The translation in *The Book of Dene,* issued by Programme Development Division, Department of Education, Yellowknife, N.W.T. (1976), has been "compared with versions in the original tongues."

shouldn't listen to outside of confession, and the comment on the Hudson's Bay Company is practically sedition; but Petitot does not hesitate to put them in. This passage is a touchstone which indicates to me that one can read Petitot with confidence.

Up to a point. Can a missionary really allow himself to place a high value on pagan mythology? In his *History of the Catholic Church in Western Canada* (1910) Father Morice does not mention that Petitot collected and published myths and legends. What is more, the role of priest as ethnologist is not dealt with at all in that two-volume history—which is quite schizophrenic, seeing that Father Morice was himself one of the greatest ethnologists of Western Canada. The situation is paradoxical. Perhaps the Church felt it could go more freely about its task of eradicating paganism if one or two of its priests recorded the old ways for posterity. Morice wrote many brilliant papers for scholarly journals, and he would figure much more prominently in our discussion here but for the fact that he published very few legends. He knew masses of them; why did he not print more?

We have no complaint about his "Three Carrier Myths" article. Indeed, it is a pleasure to hear him tell how he transcribed them:

> I have a reliable Indian narrate me as clearly as possible the whole of one myth (when this is not too long) in his native language. I then repeat as verbatim as I can what I have heard, subject to corrections when such may be necessary, and then I write down the whole in Indian. . . . As I speak Carrier more fluently than English or even than my native French, my thoughts are generally through the channel of the aboriginal idiom, so that I find no great difficulty in repeating, and afterwards in writing down in almost the same terms what has been told me. This method has also the advantage of preventing the narrative from being cut up in those short, half-line sentences common to the stories transcribed on dictation, and which some may wrongly believe to

Father Moricé, O.M.I., "à l'entrée de son jardin, félicité (mai 1933) de son élévation au grade de Docteur en Droit"; with the noted Vancouver historian, Judge Howay.

Photo courtesy of Archives Deschâtelets, Ottawa.

14

be the normal condition of Indian phraseology.[2]

Good; but why not publish more? From his commentary on the "Three Carrier Myths," it becomes clear that each was chosen for a purpose. The first is connected to the Fall and the Flood; the second to the burning of Sodom; and the third to Greek mythology (p. 35). Morice apparently desires to discover for his wards a kinship with the Mediterranean cradle of civilization, the lost tribes of Israel hinted at (p. 26). We find Petitot saying the same kind of thing: "the traditional story of Moses has been preserved in a more archaic form among the peoples of the far north. . . . We have, in the Déné-dindjié people, some of the lost remnants of Israel now converted to Catholicism" (Vol. I, p. 64). Thus, the two Catholic missionaries who are on record as attending to myth and legend have something of an axe to grind. Whether or not it affected in subtle ways what seems so authentic in Petitot is probably not susceptible of proof. Clearly, it affected Morice's choice of what myths he published. And when he defends himself against "the charge of negligence in not having, to this day, collected more than fragments" by stating that their epic is "merely a Carrier version of a myth which is the original property of the Pacific Coast Indians" (p. 1), then we are doubly disappointed. He neglects the Carrier heroic narrative because it is similar to what he has heard elsewhere: the

---

[2]"Three Carrier Myths" *Transactions of the Canadian Institute* 5 (1894-95) 1-36, quotation on pp. 3-4. The four interlined texts offered in *The Carrier Language* (1932) Vol. II have a rather apologetic introduction: "The author of this work has, in various monographs, considered the Carriers from every possible angle, and studied their ethnology, sociology, archaeology, technology, history and, now, language. One viewpoint, mythology, he may be accused of having perhaps a little neglected, because he has consecrated only one paper exclusively to it. Yet, apart from the four legends whose text is hereunder given, the following myths scattered in his works will, we think, lead one to realize that he has not altogether overlooked this part of their ancestral heirloom" (p. 513). Morice lists eleven myths, a meagre total.

argument is unworthy of him. The hidden motive must be his instinct that the old imaginative cosmology is too powerful. With their own epic intact, the Carrier would not be a lost tribe, needing to be saved.

Let us not leave the other denominations out of the discussion. The Rev. Thomas Crosby, who speaks for the Methodists in his *Among the An-ko-me-nums* (Toronto 1907), writes: "Of their [the Halkomelem] traditions we have not much to say" (p. 114). In the later autobiography, *Up and Down the North Pacific Coast by Canoe and Mission Ship* (Toronto 1914), he allows his daughter a few pages for some stories she heard as a teacher of Indian children (pp. 100-111). They are slender offerings. They might be of interest to an expert on the tribe concerned. This would be a general rule in all these cases: a scholar with vital interest in a subject will find even the most peripheral material pertinent — the smallest pieces have an essential place in his big jigsaw puzzle. Pursuing our aim of trying to find reliable texts which are interesting *in themselves,* we may have to cast aside, with ungracious haste, contributions such as Miss Jessie Crosby's.

And even the Rev. Charles Harrison's. He was the Anglican clergyman in the Queen Charlotte Islands for forty years, published a Haida grammar, and could speak to the people in their own tongue; but he used his competence in the cause of conversion only. In the chapter of *Ancient Warriors of the North Pacific* (London 1925) on the Indian's view of life after death, it is curious how precisely it reflects his own; for it is a world of the good and bad injun. The virtuous one goes to heaven: "the gates of cedar, beautifully carved and ornamented with shells, were thrown open for his admittance, and his soul, which by this time had assumed the shape of his earthly body, but clothed in ethereal light, was delivered to the Chief of Light. . . .The bad Indian, in the region of the clouds," the Rev. Harrison reports, "was suppposed to be tortured continually" (p. 126). This seems a wee bit High Church. The Raven story of Chapter XI (pp. 149-164) has merit; but there is no reason to seek out this version, unless, of course, one is working on a Haida jigsaw puzzle, in which case Harrison is quite a large piece to find a place for.

Archie Phinney and the Limits of the Printed Page

If an intelligent young man from an Indian band went to college, got good training in ethnographic techniques, and then returned home to collect and edit his tribal stories, he would, to say the least, be a better bet than your average missionary. This is what we have in the case of Archie Phinney, B.A. Kansas, 1926; graduate courses in anthropology at George Washington University, Washington, D.C.; thence to Columbia, where he had the good sense to seek out Franz Boas, who, after further training, sent him back to his home reservation in Idaho during the winter 1929-30. The result was a collection Boas considered "among the best told myths that we have from American Indians."[3] It should be emphasized that, after the first push, this was all Phinney's work: a Native ethnologist in control of every stage from field transcription to the printed page. One has to look far for anything similar; even the Osage work of Francis La Flesche did not give us a polished gem like Phinney's *Nez Percé Texts* (New York: Columbia University Press 1934).

The proceedings of the American Ethnological Society for 1976, compiled by Margot Liberty with the title *American Indian Intellectuals* (1978), has made a start on giving due prominence to the Native co-workers previously hidden in the shadow of their anthropologist employers. I intend to continue the process in this book, and introduce Archie Phinney at the head of the list. Nor should I forget *his* informant, his mother. They made a good team:

---

[3]Franz Boas, a letter of recommendation for Archie Phinney, 23 February 1934. From microfilm of the Professional Correspondence of Franz Boas, American Philosophical Society, Philadelphia. The short obituary of Phinney in *American Anthropologist* 52 (1950) 442 summarizes his career as an Indian agent, but strangely forgets his *Nez Percé Texts*.

> ... the narrator Wayilatpu, who is not conversant with the English language, felt no restraint, no unnaturalness in reproducing these tales on the basis of her excellent memory... the recorder's familiarity with the native language eliminated laborious recording and made it possible to deal expeditiously, and without artificiality and looseness, with phraseology no longer current (p. vii).

In this Introduction to the texts, Phinney is groping for a vocabulary by which to describe what he considers desirable in a well-presented tale. His concern to find a style equal to the reality of the storytelling is demonstrated further in his correspondence with Boas. "A sad thing in recording these animal stories," he writes from Idaho to New York on 20 November 1929, "is the loss of spirit—the fascination furnished by the peculiar Indian vocal rendition for humor. Indians are better storytellers than whites. When I read my story mechanically I find only the cold corpse." Boas replies that Phinney should "try to learn to tell a few stories just as lively as the Indians do and with all their gestures. We can then try once more to get it down on phonographic discs so that we get really the way a good story teller tells it. Of course you must practise on it a good deal to get it in the right, lively form" (letter 27 November 1929). "With the practice you suggest," Phinney unenthusiastically replies (3 December 1929), "I can render the subtleties of humor, derogation, exclamation, etc., if you see a way to portray this element to students lacking an understanding of the Indian habit of thought, who see mostly only symmetrical mechanics in primitive languages."

Phinney became more encouraged when he had a chance to compare his own results with others: "It is particularly gratifying to me to find in our collection a more natural spirit, higher plot unity, and generally fuller elaboration of particular incidents" (letter to Boas 5 December 1930). If we pounce on this casual statement and use it to forward our main argument, it is because one rarely finds criteria stated so succinctly and from so eximious a source:

18

(i) "natural spirit"—I take this to mean the ease of flow of words which a born story-teller has, so that his or her pleasure in the performance is communicated to the audience (and, if we can find a way to do it, to the reader) as a shared feeling of confidence and buoyancy;

(ii) "plot unity"—a beginning, a middle, and an end, encompassing an action of some scope and significance, so that, no matter how unpredictable the episodes, a good story will make them hang together to the satisfaction of the teller and his listeners;

(iii) "elaboration of particular incidents"—subtle clues to character, crucial hints about motivation, suspense sustained by attention to detail, pregnant pauses, the hidden tensions of repartee, dramatic irony: Indian legends are not famous for these qualities. Is it because we have had too many truncated versions put in front of us? Occasionally, thank goodness, we come across texts which have enticing intricacy, where the raconteur "has obtained complete mastery over his technique" and "plays" with his material.[4]

---

[4]Paul Radin *Literary Aspects of North American Mythology* Canada Geological Survey Museum Bulletin No. 16 (1915) pp. 42-43, where he adds:

> Anyone who has spent any time among Indians must have been impressed by the fact that only a few Indians in any tribe have the reputation of being excellent raconteurs. And it is a different kind of excellence with which each raconteur is credited . . . one man was famous for the humorous touches which he imparted to every tale; another, for the fluency with which he spoke and the choice of his language; a third, for his dramatic delivery; a fourth, for the radical way in which he handled time-worn themes; a fifth, for his tremendous memory; a sixth, for the accuracy with which he adhered to the "accepted" version; etc.

Phinney referred to "the striking superiority" of his mother's stories "from the point of view of native style, completeness and continuity" —continuity, here, in the sense that "these tales were handed down from one narrator to another, going back three generations" (*Nez*

The spirited flow of narrative, the coherence of the action, and the richness of detail: these are not criteria we are unfamiliar with in literary criticism. They have been basic from the beginnings of art. But we are still left with the question of the style that different people use to fulfill these criteria; and specifically the job of registering that an oral performance has accomplished what it set out to do. Much of the "play" is in the paralanguage of gesture, tone of voice, and timing. The humour, especially, is in innuendo, which involves all three. This is what worried Phinney most in presenting his tales. For all his care to find "absolute equivalents" in his literal interlinear translations, "the specific conceptual form-ations" and "the inner feel so far as it is possible to do so" (letters 16 April and 18 November 1933); for all his care to have the free translation embody "the emotional flavor or usage of words in sentences—the spirit of the tale" (16 April 1933); for all his concern to distinguish between a coyote and Coyote, a meadowlark and Meadowlark, based "on a feeling for something that inheres to animal names" (letter 26 Febru-ary 1934); for all his care to give animals their traditional speech characteristics, where "Fox always speaks with utmost clarity and directness," "Bear slurs consonants," and "Skunk nasalizes in a high-pitched voice" (Introduction, p. ix); for all this care, when it came to the essential humour of the episodes, no amount of care, he felt, could get it on to the page; and he was reduced to stating flatly in his Introduction that a certain couple of the tales are "excellent examples of the depth, and delightful flavor of Indian humor" (p. ix). He is right to worry; for these specified tales are not, on the face of it, more humourous than the general run of Coyote stories. Something

---

Percé Texts p. viii). All these judgments are valuable in building up coherent criteria for appreciating Indian myth and legend, as there have not been, to my knowledge, any recorded attempts at formal literary criticism by Native intellectuals up to the present time. I am not at all sure that ethnologists (with but one or two noted exceptions) have asked questions about the qualities that make a myth or legend attractive and enjoyable.

vital is obviously lost in transmission, and we are in danger of being left, as he feared, with the "cold corpse" of a story.[5]

Archie Phinney was a man of independent mind—witness his research in Russia (1932-36) even before the Soviet Union had diplomatic recognition from the United States. In preparing his *Nez Percé Texts,* however, he did not have the genius to go beyond the rather staid format that his mentor expected of him. He could not allow himself to think of some of the solutions to the problem of humour which we have seen attempted in recent years. For instance, Dennis Tedlock has a Coyote story in *Finding the Center* (1972), and the typographical devices for loudness, pauses, prolonged syllables, and other performance features help, I think, to convey the humour. Coyote has annoyed Old Lady Junco by repeatedly asking her for her song:

> *He was coming for the fourth time*
> *when Old Lady Junco said to herself,* (tight) *"Oh*
> > *here you come*
> *but I won't sing," that's what she said.*
> *She looked for a round rock.*
> When she found a round rock, she
> dressed it with her Junco shirt, she put her basket of
> > seeds with her Junco rock.
> (tight) *"As for you, go right ahead and ask."* (p. 81)

As one becomes familiar with Tedlock's notations, one begins to hear precisely the tone of voice which carries the humour. Coyote is going to ask for the song again; the rock, of course, is not going to say anything; and Coyote is eventually going to take a bite out of the rock at the expense of his molars. So much of the humour is in the anticipation of the outcome, and the way the hints of the outcome are allowed to leak into the narrative. Anticipatory laughter in the audience is triggered

---

[5]Dell Skeels has made a contribution with his articles, "A Classification of Humor in Nez Perce Mythology" *Journal of American Folklore* 67 (1954) 57-63, and "The Function of Humor in Three Nez Perce Indian Myths" *American Imago* 11 (1954) 249-261; but he by no means exhausts the topic.

by a laconic quality in the way the denouement is prepared.

How much laughter? In transcribing Yellowman's Coyote story, J. Barre Toelken settled the question by *stating* how much. A recording of a particular telling before several of Yellowman's children on the evening of 19 December 1966 was transcribed two years after, with the help of one of those children. It is instructive to see how early in the story the laughter begins:

> (style: slow, as with factual conversational prose; regular intonation and pronunciation; long pauses between sentences, as if tired)
>
> Ma'i [Coyote] was walking along once in a once-forested area named after a stick floating on the water. He began walking in the desert in this area, where there were many prairie dogs, and as he passed by them they called him mean names, but he ignored them. He was angry, even so, and it was noon by then, so he made a wish:
>
> (slower, all vowels more nasalized) "I wish some clouds would form." He was thinking about killing these prairie dogs, so he wished for clouds, and there were clouds. (audience: smiles and silent laughter)[6]

The children know that Coyote wants rain so that he can pretend to be drowned in the flood, so that he can get Skunk to bring the prairie dogs to gloat over his "corpse," and then he can jump them. They are already smiling at the way this circuitous plan is initiated. The mimicry and the special animal voice probably have something to do with this early laughter; and also the feeling that their father is not going to rush the story—it is going to be told well. Toelken's transcription indicates the different kinds of laughter, including Yellowman's

---

[6]J. Barre Toelken "The 'Pretty Language' of Yellowman: Genre, Mode, and Texture in Navaho Coyote Narratives" *Genre* 2 (1969) 211-235, quotation pp. 215-216.

own laughter at certain points. There are also footnotes to explain certain comic devices, and an extended commentary which shows the social importance of the humour. It is a very full treatment of a performance text, one which Archie Phinney, I think, would have appreciated. It might be too cumbersome for everyday use — though I am not so sure about that.[7] In any case, it allows us to go back to texts like Phinney's, and understand how they "reveal currents of subtle humor" (Introduction p. ix), and why Phinney in a letter can state that "Indians are better storytellers than whites" without expecting to be contradicted.

"A Masterpiece of Indian Oral Tradition"

It is instructive to look briefly at the recent *Nez Perce Texts* (University of California Press 1979), not only to note that Archie Phinney has not suffered disesteem at the hands of a contemporary specialist in the field, but also to see what sorts of things the editor, Haruo Aoki, feels should be included nowadays to give proper support to a text. Aoki does not lean toward the techniques of Tedlock or Toelken. There is merely the Native text with literal interlinear translation, followed by a free translation. But he is careful to add biographical information on the informants, including photographs; a

---

[7]Since the above was written Toelken has surprised us with a new rendition of Yellowman's story, published with Tacheeni Scott (a Navajo Ph.D. candidate in biology at the University of Oregon) as "Poetic Retranslation and the 'Pretty Languages' of Yellowman" in Karl Kroeber ed. *Traditional Literatures of the American Indian* (Lincoln: University of Nebraska Press 1981) pp. 65-116. New devices are used, which further the aims of the original article. The pace of exploration into the various ways of transcribing performance is quickening. One excellent example is *Linguistic Convergence: An Ethnology of Speaking at Fort Chipewyan, Alberta* (New York: Academic Press 1979), where Ronald and Suzanne Scollon's indebtedness to Toelken is expressed and clearly evident. (Note that the book is a somewhat expanded version of Ronald Scollon's monograph in the Mercury Series, National Museums of Canada 1979, *The Context of the Informant Narrative Performance*.)

23

statement of the circumstances in which the stories were recorded; and ethnographic notes on certain details, on the significance of the story as a whole, and on its position in the widespread themes of world mythology. This is all in keeping with the trend to provide context for the "raw material"— "raw" being Viola Garfield's word for an objectionable severity in the way most ethnographers had presented their collections of myths up to the time of her "Contemporary Problems of Folklore Collecting and Study" in 1953. This was a milestone article;[8] as Melville Jacobs' *The Content and Style of an Oral Literature* was a further milestone in 1959. The trend, of which the 1979 *Nez Perce Texts* is a good recent result, is characterized by a concern for the narrator and his precise purposes, and for providing enough comment on the narrator's skills and audience reactions, so that a literary judgment might one day be made. Jacobs thought such judgments

---

[8]In *Alaska University, Anthropological Papers,* Vol. I (May 1953) pp. 25-36. It is a useful survey, with a well-selected bibliography, of previous scholars who have attempted to discuss and portray the "dynamic factors in myth making" (p. 26). One of the earliest of these was Bronislaw Malinowski, whose essay "Myth in Primitive Psychology" (1926) is now conveniently available in Anchor paperback, *Magic, Science and Religion* ed. Robert Redfield (1948) pp. 93-148, where we find the following pertinent passage:

The whole nature of the performance, the voice and the mimicry, the stimulus and the response of the audience mean as much to the natives as the text; and the sociologist should take his cue from the natives. The performance, again, has to be placed in its proper time setting—the hour of the day, and the season, with the background of the sprouting gardens awaiting future work, and slightly influenced by the magic of the fairy tales. We must also bear in mind the sociological context of private ownership, the sociable function and the cultural role of amusing fiction. All these elements are equally relevant; all must be studied as well as the text. The stories live in native life and not on paper, and when a scholar jots them down without being able to evoke the atmosphere in which they flourish he has given us but a mutilated bit of reality (p. 104).

"premature" (p. 8); Catharine McClellan provided another milestone when in 1970 she published *The Girl Who Married the Bear* (National Museum of Man, Publications in Ethnology, No. 2) and termed it "a masterpiece."

She confesses that the bear-bride story at first interested her in a very limited way, as merely one more statistic in the distribution of bear ceremonialism. Then she began to ask why: why this story's great popularity? Value judgments followed. She saw that it was "an outstanding piece of creative narrative":

> For the first time I began to realize that many of the Indian myths that I had been reading in professional collections were more than rather one-dimensional "fairy stories." Today I believe that this particular story attracts the Southern Yukon natives with the same power as does a first-rate psychological drama or novel in our own culture. The themes probably evoke the same intense response in the Indians as those evoked in the Greeks by the great Attic dramas (p. 1).

Catharine McClellan is here saying that Northwest Native Indian myths are as great as Greek tragedy within their own social context. Even if she were only fifty percent right, her statement would still be magnificent; and manifold in its implications. Mythographers have now come of age, and can make judgments about these materials, which have suffered because of our timidity. There is now one "masterpiece," and there will be others.

Moreover, myth-critics have a special role in this. It is not only that some stories will be judged more powerful than others on the grounds of style and substance, but also that what one is essentially judging cannot usually be a single text but a continuum where storytellers have "thrown" versions of a story, like several potters trying for the same shape of pot. Catharine McClellan's subtitle, "A Masterpiece of Indian Oral Tradition," refers to no one telling of "The Girl Who

Married the Bear," but to the eleven versions of it which together give it scope, and by means of which the scholar can discern a pan-tribal artifact of fullness, coherence, and beauty. She is eager to talk about the personality of an informant and the way special circumstances in the situation may have contributed to the details of a story.[9] She is very much within the modern trend here. But this concern with differences does not lead her to pick out the best telling as *the* masterpiece, but to take the term we usually reserve for the finest work of an individual master and apply it to something she herself, in effect, has created, a "story" enlarged beyond the sum total of the different tellings. The mythographer sees and appreciates a whole denied to individual raconteurs.

No other mythographer has yet undertaken the task of "creating" a masterpiece myth in exactly this sense. Dell Hymes, an anthropologist and linguist, has been moving, with due deliberation, into the role of literary critic of myth, and has now collected pertinent papers into a volume, *"In vain I tried to tell you"* (Philadelphia: University of Pennsylvania Press 1981). This volume constitutes a clear announcement that, in Hymes's opinion, the oral tradition in North America (as, indeed, mostly elsewhere) was a verse tradition, and that this is revealed by minute attention to extant texts. Jarold W. Ramsey, a younger Oregonian follower of Hymes and a professor of English, has the distinction of having introduced North American Indian myth analysis into the august pages of *PMLA*.[10] In their sensitive approach to a handful of classic published texts, Hymes and Ramsey have, in a sense, elevated

---

[9]It is clear that McClellan and her teacher Frederica de Laguna have a meeting of minds on the importance of context in presenting a tale, see de Laguna's *Under Mount Saint Elias: The History and Culture of the Yakutat Tlingit* (Washington, D.C.: Smithsonian Institution 1972), especially "The Story of the Woman Who Married a Bear" pp. 880-882.

[10]Jarold W. Ramsey "The Wife Who Goes Out like a Man, Comes Back as a Hero: The Art of Two Oregon Indian Narratives" *PMLA* 92 (January 1977) 9-18. Ramsey's recent "From 'Mythic' to

them beyond what the original teller and recorder would have claimed for them. This is not unusual in literary criticism, which is always at work to transform a bewildering multiplicity of blocks and pieces into a corpus of literature, within the coherent framework of which they can be better understood, enjoyed, and judged. The stage is set for the entry of North American Indian myth and legend into a much larger role in the pageant of world literatures.

We have gone somewhat outside our chosen area of British Columbia to take a look at a number of missionary collectors of legend, the exceptional work of one full-blooded Native ethnologist, and the advance-guard of the growing movement to treat Indian storytelling as a major literature. The issues raised will be hovering continually over our subsequent discussion. I will not be telling the history of myth-collecting in British Columbia without bias. I am biased in favour of what Petitot did, what Archie Phinney did, and what Catharine McClellan did. I instinctively recognize what they did as authentic; and their work helps me to define the term. It has something to do with the ethnologist's honest care for the storyteller and his or her people; with recognizing a born raconteur when one hears one; with valuing the dramatic elements of a story at least as much as the linguistic and ethnographic; and with striving for techniques to bring the living story on to the printed page.

'Fictive' in a Nez Percé Orpheus Myth" appears in *Traditional Literatures of the American Indian* ed. Karl Kroeber (1981) pp. 24-44.

Chapter II
Before Boas

In the summer of 1896 Charles Hill-Tout, an immigrant schoolteacher newly arrived in Vancouver, took a boat across Burrard Inlet to the Squamish Mission village in what is now North Vancouver. Bishop Durieu had prepared the way, and the chief men of the tribe soon brought the visitor to the old, blind "historian," Mulks. "I first sought to learn his age," says Hill-Tout, "but this he could only approximately give by informing me that his mother was a girl on the verge of womanhood when Vancouver sailed up Howe Sound at the close of the last century. He would, therefore, be about 100 years old."[1] What Hill-Tout then witnessed is, as far as I know, unique in the annals of myth collecting on the Northwest Coast of America: this Squamish "Homer" proceeded to orate the epic of the origin of his people as though in a formal ceremonial occasion.

> Before the old man could begin his recital, some
> preparations were deemed necessary by the other
> elderly men of the tribe. These consisted in making
> a bundle of short sticks, each about six inches long.

---

[1] *The Salish People: The Local Contribution of Charles Hill-Tout* ed. Ralph Maud (Vancouver: Talonbooks 1978) Vol. II p. 19.

These played the part of tallies, each stick repre-
senting to the reciter a particular paragraph or
chapter in his story. They apologized for making
these, and were at pains to explain to me that these
were to them what books were to the white man.
These sticks were now placed at intervals along a
table round which we sat, and after some animated
discussion between the interpreter, who acted as
master of ceremonies, and the other old men as to
the relative order and names of the tallies, we were
ready to begin. The first tally was placed in the old
man's hands and he began his recital in a loud,
high-pitched key, as if he were addressing a large
audience in the open air. He went on without pause
for about ten minutes, and then the interpreter
took up the story. The story was either beyond the
interpreter's power to render into English, or there
was much in it he did not like to relate to a white
man, for I did not unfortunately get a fifth of what
the old man had uttered from him, and it was only
by dint of questioning and cross-questioning that I
was enabled to get anything like a connected
narrative from him at all. The old man recited his
story chapter by chapter, that is, tally by tally, and
the interpreter followed in like order (pp. 19-20).

In his paper communicated to the Royal Society of Canada in
1897, Hill-Tout presents as much of this Squamish Flood story
as he was able to record. In spite of the difficulties, it is more
detailed than the large majority of such origin stories. Most
important to our mythographic concerns are a couple of
notes that Hill-Tout adds about the actual performance. Mulks
is telling how "the Great Spirit" punished the tribe with an
especially crippling kind of snowstorm: "In this part of his
recital the old man was exceedingly interesting and graphic in
his description, the very tones of his voice lending themselves
to his story, and I gathered, long before the interpreter took

Charles Hill-Tout, the frontispiece photograph to his volume, *Man and his Ancestors in the Light of Organic Evolution* (Vancouver 1925).

up the story, that he had told of something that was very small and had penetrated everywhere" (p. 21). Starvation and cold caused the death of hundreds, and here "the old man's voice was hushed to a plaintive wail, and the faces of his audience were an eloquent index of the tragic interest of this story of their ancestors' misfortunes" (p. 21). When so much of what we have of Native myth is little more than a minimal report of how the story used to be told, it is refreshing to have the sense of a "performance": Mulks is truly "on stage."[2] Hill-Tout's inexperience worked in his favour here. If he had been better trained he would have taken Mulks aside and got the original Squamish down by slow dictation; instead, we get a picture of something that might have happened before any white man came on the scene.

Franz Boas was working on the Coast by 1886, quite a few years before Hill-Tout's arrival. But chronology does not count. Hill-Tout is "Before Boas" in the naivete with which he began his work. His background was rural England, a Church of England upbringing. He might have become a clergyman but for some "intellectual difficulties" of a Darwinian sort. He arrived in Toronto in 1884 with a letter of introduction to Dr. (later Sir) Daniel Wilson, and must have seemed just the kind of "young Dominion man" Wilson had prophesied would "arise to bear a part in letters and science not less worthy than those who figure on England's golden roll."[3] Wilson spoke to him of "the vanishing race" and the opportunities for anthropological research in the West. When a sequence of circumstances brought Hill-Tout to settle in Vancouver in 1891 he was ready and eager to do his bit. His residence in the area gave him the advantage of being able to renew by continued visits the friendships he made with local Indians.

He had an interest in spiritualism, as did John Swanton; but I do not know that Swanton gained an insight into the visionary

---

[2]Dell Hymes defines true performance as "the taking of responsibility for being 'on stage'"—see his "Folklore's Nature and the Sun's Myth" *Journal of American Folklore* 88 (1975) 352.

[3]*The Salish People* Vol. I p. 13.

experience in quite the direct manner that Hill-Tout did. In a report to the Society for Psychical Research in London in 1895, Hill-Tout tells of the seances being conducted in Vancouver and his own shaman-like experience at one of them. Like a spirit-dance song, the hymn "Nearer, my God, to Thee" induced in him "strange sensations":

> I stood up and began to sway to and fro, and soon lost all sense of my surroundings. I seemed to be far away in space. The feelings of distance and remoteness from all other beings were very marked, and a sense of coldness and loneliness oppressed me terribly. I seemed to be moving, or rather to be drawn downward, and presently felt that I had reached this earth again; but all was strange and fearful and lonely, and I seemed to be disappointed that I could not attain the object of this long and lonely journey. I felt I was looking for someone, but did not seem to have a clear notion of whom it was, and as the hopelessness of my search and the fruitlessness of my long journey forced itself upon me, I cried out in my wretchedness and misery. I felt I could neither find what I wanted nor get back from whence I had come. My grief was very terrible, and I should have fallen to the ground but that the other sitters had gathered round me. . . . [4]

The Native gaining of a guardian spirit is not dissimilar, in essence. Hill-Tout's Indian friends must have had some sense of this:

> It was not till Captain Paul [of the Lillooet tribe] and I had spent several weeks in each other's company and I had won his confidence and esteem and he had bestowed upon me one of his ancestral mystery names, thereby relating me to himself, that he gave me . . . esoteric information concerning the

---

[4]*The Salish People* Vol. IV p. 60.

abnormal sight powers he claimed to have formerly possessed. I do not, for my own part, doubt his possession of them for a moment.[5]

Such a profound relationship between Indian and white is rarely so convincingly documented. It makes for good story collecting.

Hill-Tout's most productive friendship was with Chief Mischèlle of Lytton, one of the most talented and informed people that a beginning field worker could ever hope to meet. Having acted as interpreter for many years to the missionaries, and also in the law courts, Mischelle was quite fluent in English. "My method of recording was as follows," writes Hill-Tout by way of preface to a single *masterpiece,* which takes up over twenty pages of small type. "I made copious notes at the time, and expanded them immediately after. When written out, I read them to him and corrected them where necessary according to his instructions."[6] This methodology may not seem very promising; but the result is the most readable body of Native literature in the canon. "Mischelle was a good raconteur, and took the liveliest pleasure in relating to me his store of lore." Hill-Tout won a prize of $25 from the Folklore Society of Montreal for the story in question; it is certainly, as "performance," worth the price of admission.

When he gains some proficiency in the Salish languages, Hill-Tout provides interlinear texts, so that we can test his free translations against them. He consistently heightens the diction to make a story warmer and more heartfelt. He likes to add adjectives. For instance, in the Squamish story of the origin of the "Wildmen," a chief's daughter is made pregnant by a slave; then, according to the interlinear literal translation:

> when he-finds-out the father, then he-takes-into the canoe the daughter-his and the slave.

---

[5] *The Salish People* Vol. II p. 122.
[6] *The Salish People* Vol. I p. 21.

Chief Mischelle of Lytton. Photograph annotated: "Michel, Head Chief of Nekla-kap-amuks, May 1879."

Hill-Tout's free translation reads: "And, on learning who it was who had caused this disgrace to fall upon him, he took both the guilty slave and his hapless daughter away in his canoe."[7] If this sounds like Victorian melodrama, it is because Hill-Tout is trying to meet fully the melodrama of the original: Indian daughters are sometimes never told to darken doorsteps again. He knows that the hearers of this story were moved by it, and he wants us to be likewise moved. This is the perennial problem. Hill-Tout's way of meeting it is to supply the emotive adjectives which the storyteller would imply in his manner:

> . . . although nothing is more wearisome than consecutive reading of collections of Indian texts, there is nothing wearisome in listening to the recital of these by the Indian himself. Most Indians possess natural dramatic powers, and their ready, graceful and appropriate gestures, and their command of those tones of the voice that appeal to the emotions, make it distinctly pleasurable to listen to their stories of long ago or their recitals of the traditions of their people. So that if the English equivalents of my native texts in this or in former reports seem fuller than the baldness of their expressions justifies, it must be understood that this is because the bare text alone does not render the full meaning and context of the living recital or do justice to the subject treated of. I have seen women shed tears, and men's faces grow pale and tense over the recital, by some of the elders of the tribe, of the traditions of the people, the text of which would make one marvel that such bald dry statements could call forth so much emotion.[8]

---

[7] *The Salish People* Vol. II p. 97. The interlinear translation may be found in the original *Report of the British Association for the Advancement of Science;* for reference, see *The Salish People* Vol. II p. 27.

[8] *The Salish People* Vol. III p. 156.

Hill-Tout is quite clear on Native showmanship, and his own.

As a member of the Ethnological Survey of Canada Committee, Hill-Tout issued full ethnological reports to the British Association for the Advancement of Science on the Thompson (1899), the Squamish (1900), the Mainland Halkomelem (1902), continuing with similar scholarly reports in the *Journal of the Royal Anthropological Institute* on the Sechelt (1904), the Chehalis and Scowlitz (1904), the Lillooet (1905), the South-Eastern Tribes of Vancouver Island (1907), and the Okanagan (1911). This work involved the collection and publication of grammars and vocabularies for eight quite different Salish languages, material which linguists today find useful. All this was accomplished in spare time during his years as a teacher in Vancouver and then, from 1899, when he moved out to the farm he had purchased in Abbotsford, in time wrested from business and family. It was a life-long grievance that he never received employment or proper recognition from academic Anthropology. It goes back to the rebuff from Boas, the exact nature of which we do not know. Hill-Tout and Boas met in Vancouver on 3 June 1897. Hill-Tout gave Boas five skulls, "one of them very valuable."[9] And that's all we know. Hill-Tout had certain expectations. He had written Boas a long letter on 3 October 1895, and Boas had replied: "It is very likely I shall be on the coast about the month of May and should be very glad if I could assist you in your interesting work. I may be able to obtain funds for this purpose."[10] Hill-Tout had rejoined: "I am exceedingly enthusiastic over the whole question and would like nothing better than to devote the next ten years of my life to the work in this district." Boas had now finally arrived on the coast; the Jesup Expedition was well financed; but Hill-Tout was not taken on. Something about Hill-Tout annoyed Boas, his tone, his

---

[9]Franz Boas, letter to Mrs. Boas, 3 June 1897, in *The Ethnology of Franz Boas* ed. Ronald P. Rohner (1969) p. 201. See *The Salish People* Vol. I p. 15.

[10]The exchange of letters between Boas and Hill-Tout is printed in *The Salish People* Vol. IV pp. 35-40.

intellectual demeanour, his presumption.[11] The result was that Hill-Tout was never published in the nice hard-cover volumes of the Jesup Expedition, nor in the Bureau of American Ethnology Bulletins, nor in the publications of the American Folklore Society, nor in any of the influential series of Anthropological volumes emanating from Columbia University. Hill-Tout's field reports never got a Library of Congress catalogue number, and thus were condemned to oblivion, or at least an eighty-year delay.

George M. Dawson could have made a great deal of difference, and his premature death in 1901 is lamentable. He was the son of the Principal of McGill, and a brilliant geologist. As a member of the staff of the Geological Survey of Canada, he overcame his physical disability, the result of polio at the age of eleven, and made many arduous explorations of the Northwest, and also did three substantial ethnographic reports in the midst of his cartography: on the Haida (1880), the Kwakiutl (1887), and the Shuswap (1891). Dawson included Mythology sections in each of these reports.[12] They are interesting as being very much "Before Boas"; but he is essentially reporting on the stories rather than presenting them. What we lost with Dawson's death is not so much a

---

[11]Boas's letter to R.W. Brock of 1910—see footnote 9 of Chapter VI (below)—refers to Hill-Tout as having "a most remarkable ability of exasperating everyone with whom he comes into contact."

[12]"On the Haida Indians of the Queen Charlotte Islands" *Report of Progress, Geological Survey of Canada, 1878-79* (Ottawa 1880) pp. 103B-179B, "Traditions and Folklore" section pp. 149B-154B; "Notes and Observations on the Kwakiool People of the Northern Part of Vancouver Island and Adjacent Coasts, made during the Summer of 1885" *Transactions of the Royal Society of Canada* 5 (1887) Sect. II pp. 63-98, myths on pp. 81-87; "Notes on the Shuswap People of British Columbia" *Transactions of the Royal Society of Canada* 9 (1891) Sect. II pp. 3-44, "Mythology" pp. 28-35. A concise discussion of Dawson's contribution to Pacific Coast ethnology is John J. Van West "George Mercer Dawson: An Early Canadian Anthropologist" *Anthropological Journal of Canada* 14 (1976) No. 4 pp. 8-12.

great story collector as a great enabler. He enabled Boas to get started on his very first season in the field, as their exchange of highly practical letters reveals.[13] He was on the Committee of the British Association for the Advancement of Science that hired Boas for his second field trip (1888) and five subsequent trips. He was the Chairman of the Association's new Committee for the Ethnographic Survey of Canada in 1897, nominating Hill-Tout for membership. Here was a man big enough to sponsor a multiplicity of attitudes and modes in anthropological research. If he had lived, the Anthropological Division which was established in 1910 within the Geological Survey would surely have been a more catholic and at the same time a more Canadian entity. As it was, Boas was consulted, and a staunch Boas man, Edward Sapir, appointed as head of the new Division. The "Canadian pioneers" were, in the words of Marius Barbeau, "virtually eliminated."[14]

---

[13]Excerpts included in Jacob W. Gruber "Horatio Hale and the Development of American Anthropology" *Proceedings of the American Philosophical Society* 111 (February 1967) 5-37, specifically pp. 21-22.

[14]Marius Barbeau "Charles Hill-Tout (1859-1944)" *Transactions of the Royal Society of Canada* 39 (1945) Sect. II pp. 89-92, an astute evaluation of early Canadian anthropology. See also Douglas Cole "The Origins of Canadian Anthropology, 1850-1910" *Journal of Canadian Studies* 8 (February 1973) 33-45. I am indebted to Douglas Cole for directing my attention to a letter from Hill-Tout to Sapir of 26 February 1912 in the National Museums of Canada (Canadian Ethnological Service), which sums up the feelings of those who were passed over:

Bucklands
Abbotsford, B.C.
Feby 26   1912

Dr. Edward Sapir
  Dom Geo Survey
    Ottawa

Dear Sir,

  I beg to acknowledge and thank you for the copies of your papers which you were kind enough to send me. Permit me to say that I heard of your appointment as

There was one Canadian pioneer who, it is safe to say, got all the recognition he deserved. At the World's Fair in Chicago, 1893, "a massive Scotchman, as rugged as his native climate, 65 years of age, with iron gray hair and beard," lorded it over the miniature Haida village he had set up there and gave daily "readings from the totem poles," telling and retelling "the

ethnologist-in-charge at Ottawa with great interest and pleasure, and I look forward to see the dreams some of us have indulged in during the last twenty years accomplished by your self and colleagues. I see only one thing to regret and that is that your survey of the anthropological problems in your paper in "Science" and the tone there adopted by you may alienate the sympathies of some of the earlier students and associations devoted to the study of the aborigines of the Dominion. You seem to have overlooked the work and efforts, or rather you seem to fail to appreciate the work and efforts of those who have endeavoured to keep alive an interest in anthropological study. I will instance one person's work only, Father Morice's. His methods may not be ideal but there is no question of his knowledge of what he writes. I question if there is another student in America with a more perfect and critical knowledge of a native tongue than F. Morice has of Carrier and cognate tongues. Yet your mention of him and his work is only a "patronizing" one in a footnote. I cannot think you are aware of the amount of pioneer work which has been done in this country, and Canadians are very touchy. I could wish you had laid a little more stress upon the value of these efforts as far as they go. You don't want to alienate any one with anthropological interest. There is so little of it shown in this country, and when you remember it took some of us over 20 years to educate the authorities at Ottawa, even with Dr. G.M. Dawson and his distinguished father Sir William's assistance, to appreciate the value and importance of anthropological studies, you will see it is indiscrete to start your work by rousing feelings of antagonism to yourself.

You will pardon my freedom in speaking but I have your work at heart and would be sorry to see any obstacles placed in your way. The next time you have an opportunity try and smooth down these ruffled feelings your paper quaint old stories connected with them."[15] The crowds of "admiring listeners" kept asking him for a book, so he went home and put together *Tales from the Totems of the Hidery* (1899).

Home was Victoria, B.C., called Fort Victoria when James Deans arrived there in January 1853 off the Puget Sound Agricultural Company's barge, "Norman Morrison." Thus, Deans had begun his field work more than thirty years "before Boas"—as a farmer in the midst of the Indians, and then, with the aid of Chinook, as an amateur ethnologist among the many tribes represented at the Fort. "I was surprised to find that each nation had a wonderful mythology. . . . My next step was to collect all I could find and write it down, in order to preserve it from oblivion" (p. 6). During 1869-70 he was on the Queen Charlotte Islands, building a tramway for the shipping of coal. He was there again in 1879, and began spending a few weeks every fall among the Haidas. In the summer of 1883, starting from Skidegate, he visited most of the villages by canoe. Between 1887 and 1899 he published seven stories in the *Journal of American Folklore*, and many small pieces in the *American Antiquarian,* all of which found their place in *Tales from the Totems of the Hidery,* though sometimes with interesting variants. For, even when the informant is named in one instance ("Mr. George Cunningham,

---

has aroused.

Yours truly,

C. Hill-Tout

Sapir apparently did not reply to this letter. When President Wesbrook of the University of British Columbia asked Sapir's advice on Hill-Tout as a candidate for the Headship of the Department of Anthropology, Sapir wrote: "To be perfectly frank, I do not think Mr. Hill-Tout would altogether answer the needs of a university" (letter of 29 June 1916, in Museums of Canada, Ethnology Division).

[15]"Archaeological Exhibits at the Fair: James Deans and his Company of Indians" *American Antiquarian* 15 (1893) 185; see James Deans, Introduction to *Tales from the Totems of the Hidery,* Vol. II of the Archives of the International Folk-Lore Association (Chicago 1899) p. 5.

James Deans of Victoria, presumably around 1893.

of Port Essington"), and even though Deans states flatly that he has given it "as near to the original as I can remember" (p. 37), the prior publication in the *Journal of American Folklore* 4 (1891) 32-33 differs so much as to suggest that neither comes very near the original. For example, at one point the love-struck hero is ordered by the cruel maiden to cut his hair short like a slave's:

> Hearing this last request he hesitated, well knowing the consequences; however, after a while he went and had it cut, and presented himself, in order to claim his reward. When she saw him she said: "You fool! to cut your hair for a woman, and become like a slave . . . ."

In the book ten years later, this passage becomes:

> No doubt, when Sun Cloud heard this last request, he had a hard struggle within himself, a struggle between true love and dishonor. Reaching home, true love prevailed. He went to a friend's house and had a close cut. Afterwards hoping all would be well he went over to her house, in order to claim his reward. As soon as she saw what he had done for her love, she said, "You fool, do you think I would wed a slave?"

At least one of these is an embroidery upon the "original"— possibly both. Deans obviously had fun travelling the country he loved, picking up these yarns, and getting them published. We would be well advised, also, to treat them as fun.

What else is there "Before Boas"? Very little. One collection of legends is of special interest not only because of its early date. *History and Folklore of the Cowichan Indians* (Victoria 1901) is a charming book compiled by Martha Douglas Harris, the daughter of Governor James Douglas by his part-Cree wife.[16] The stories are presented lightly and modestly.

> As a little girl I used to listen to these legends with the greatest delight, and in order not to lose them, I have written down what I can remember of them. When written down they lose their charm which was in the telling. They need the quaint songs and the sweet voice that told them, the winter gloaming and the bright fire as the only light—then were these legends beautiful (p. 57).

This book contains a rare item, the transcription of a story in Chinook jargon, followed by a translation (pp. 43-49).[17]

G.M. Sproat was an early homesteader before he became a well-known government representative in Indian affairs. There is legend material in Sproat's *Scenes and Studies of Savage Life* (London 1868),[18] among the earliest recorded for this area. In a footnote to the mythology chapter (p. 177) Sproat mentions the Rev. A.C. Garrett of Victoria, and the "active and observant traveller," Dr. Robert Brown, as both possessing "extensive information on this subject." Brown's known publications do not include mythology,[19] and the Rev. Garrett did not apparently publish at all.

It would perhaps put things in perspective to mention that the classic Alaskan ethnology is Aurel Krause's *The Tlingit*

---

[16]See Derek Pethick *James Douglas: Servant of Two Empires* (Vancouver: Mitchell Press 1969) pp. 266-273, though there is no mention of Martha's collection of myths.

[17]Melville Jacobs *Texts in Chinook Jargon* (University of Washington Publications in Anthropology, Vol. 7 No. 1, November 1936) pp. 1-27 includes some stories in Chinook jargon from Thomas Paul of Saanich, collected in Victoria in May 1930.

[18]Extracts from this early book were included in Tom McFeat's paperback compilation, *Indians of the North Pacific Coast* (Toronto: McClelland and Stewart 1966); but these did not include Sproat's mythology chapter.

[19]Wayne Suttles in a personal communication corrects me on this point. One of Brown's publications which I have been unable to locate contains a "star-husband" tale.

Indians, first published in Jena in 1885, translated by Erna Gunther in 1956, and available in a University of Washington paperback since 1970. Chapter 10 contains several well-authenticated legends, including some from previous explorers, Veniaminof, Lisiansky, and Lütke. The latter's *Voyage autour du monde, 1826-1829,* published in Paris in 1835, takes us back into the early nineteenth century.[20]

---

[20]The Norwegian brothers Adrian and Fillip Jacobsen lived on the West Coast for a number of years, especially at Bella Coola, and wrote a few reports for German periodicals in the period 1890-1895. These have been collected and translated by the B.C. Indian Language Project, and await publication. What we have seen in English have been the few myths included by Boas in his *Mythology of the Bella Coola Indians* (1898). Notable among the material supplied by early explorers and travelers is "Report on the Indian Tribes inhabiting the country in the vicinity of the 49th Parallel of North Latitude" published by Capt. E.E. Wilson of the Boundary Survey in *Transactions of the Ethnological Society of London* 4 (1866) 275-322, which includes one vigorously told Coyote story.

Chapter III
Franz Boas: Early Field Work

"There is little on public record or floating in tradition regarding the youth of Boas," reports A.L. Kroeber in the festschrift published by the American Anthropological Association in the year after Boas's death in 1942.[1] There is no youthful dream which it was his life's goal to fulfill. His enormous energy and output seem not to have been attached to a single dominating insight, but to have been austerely empirical. Any general statement could only be enunciated when data gave statistical proof. He resisted Hitler propaganda on the racial question with all the power of his mature authority; but the world does not associate the name of Boas with "racial equality," as it does Darwin's with "evolution," Marx's with "communism," and Freud's with "the unconscious." Even by the end of his

---

[1] A.L. Kroeber "Franz Boas: The Man," pp. 5-26 of A.L. Kroeber et al *Franz Boas 1858-1942* (1943), published as an issue of the *American Anthropologist* Vol. 45; quotation on p. 5. This admirable biographical piece makes it unnecessary to go elsewhere for general information about Boas's life. Boas himself gives a gracious account of his entry into Anthropology in the Introduction to *The Kwakiutl of Vancouver Island* (1909).

long working life, the proofs were not in. "He made no one great summating discovery," says Kroeber (p. 24). Up to the end he was sifting the materials.

Boas was born in Minden, Westphalia, on 9 July 1858, to Meier Boas, a prosperous businessman, and his wife Sophie, a founder of the first Froebel Kindergarten in Minden and one of a circle of intellectuals "of the Mosaic confession" (as Boas once phrased it). Perhaps the most significant event in his life occurred in the fallow years after his doctorate, when he was waiting for some position. The event is of a personal nature. His aunt's husband, Dr. Abraham Jacobi of New York City, invited Franz for a holiday in the Hartz mountains. Marie Krackowizer was of the party, one of two daughters accompanied by their mother, the widow of an Austrian doctor who had emigrated to the United States after the troubles of 1848. If Boas was to marry Marie, as he immediately knew he must, he had to have a career, and in the United States to boot. We can see Boas's early ambition as half scientific thrust and half the securing of a lady's hand in marriage. His letter-diaries make it quite clear where he would have preferred to be rather than on the S.S. Boskowitz up and down the Northwest Coast. Field work was not an enjoyable way of life, but merely a means of providing the raw materials for linguistic and statistical analysis, which could be conducted in the comfort of his own study at home. This not only explains the rather limited amount of time he spent in the field and the welcome he gave to informants who, when properly trained, could mail to New York quite usable information, but also illuminates Boas's general moral stance: his life in New York, his editing, his teaching, and his marriage, this was so successful and satisfying that other ways of life, it seems, could only be looked down upon. Crime, casual sexuality, roisterous play, religious anxiety or enthusiasm, pastimes, or any form of unemployment, these were things he did not know much about, didn't want to know much about. Perhaps one reason why the principle of equality was never powerfully enough enunciated is that he could not really believe that another

48

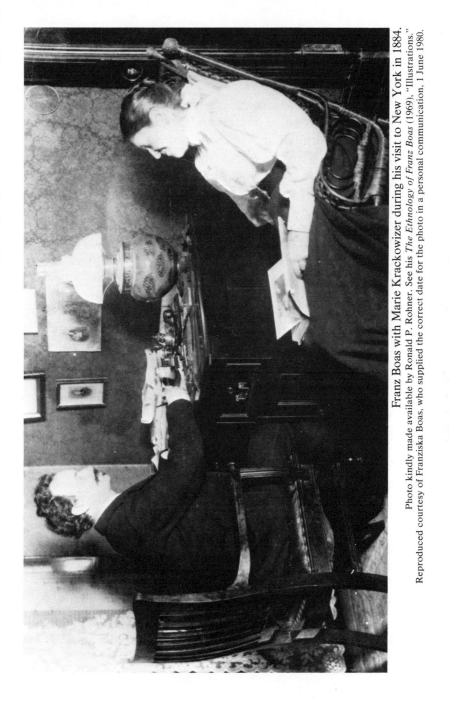

Franz Boas with Marie Krackowizer during his visit to New York in 1884.
Photo kindly made available by Ronald P. Rohner. See his *The Ethnology of Franz Boas* (1969), "Illustrations." Reproduced courtesy of Franziska Boas, who supplied the correct date for the photo in a personal communication, 1 June 1980.

49

mode of life might be as good as the one he was fortunate enough to possess.

Indianische Sagen

It is rather dismaying to the general reader that the first major publication of myths and legends of the Northwest Coast was printed in German in 1895 and has remained untranslated.[2] *Indianische Sagen von der Nord-Pacifische Küste Amerikas* is a collection of the stories published during 1888-1895 in the two German periodicals hospitable to Boas's reports, the gatherings from his first four trips to British Columbia, 1886, 1888, 1889, and 1890. The itineraries for these field trips have been conveniently tabulated and summarized in Ronald P. Rohner's "Franz Boas: Ethnographer on the Northwest Coast" ed. June Helm *Pioneers of American Anthropology* (1966) pp. 151-247. What is also dismaying is how hurriedly these stories were collected. Outside of his base in Victoria, Boas never spent more than two weeks at any one place, often only a day or two. He worked under severe financial restrictions and faced many obstacles, the chief of which, initially, was his own inexperience. He had been a year with Eskimos in Baffinland (1883-84), and his observations there went far beyond his formal function of geographer, as *The Central Eskimo* (1888) attests. But the only Indians he had seen before 1886 were the Bella Coola "exhibited" at the Berlin Museum the previous year. Boas had taken the opportunity to do "field" research with this group,

---

[2]The British Columbia Indian Language Project has arranged for an authorized translation to be prepared by Dietrich Bertz and edited for future publication by Randy Bouchard and Dorothy I.D. Kennedy. I am indebted to them for making available to me a typescript of this translation, *Indian Myths and Legends from the North Pacific Coast of America* (copyright 1977).

Later note: Columbia University Press have accepted this volume for early publication. Several selections from the *Sagen* have been published in a periodical—see footnote to p. 184 below.

and had published on their language and culture.[3] As it happened, a couple of these very Bella Coola contacts were in Victoria when he arrived on 18 September 1886, and facilitated his movements among the resident and visiting Indians. Speed was essential; he had budgeted for only three months to do a general reconnaissance of all the coastal tribes. "I am as well known here in Victoria as a mongrel dog," he wrote of this period. "I look up all kinds of people without modesty or hesitation."[4] We can share his sense of depravity at trying to obtain clean texts in the congested Indian slums, and it is refreshing to read that, after sixteen days of hustling, he has embarked on a boat going north. He spends 6-17 October 1886 in Nawitti at the furthest tip of Vancouver Island. After 18-23 October at Alert Bay, he is back in Victoria for 26 October to 2 November; then off again to Cowichan (4-10 November); Comox (12 November to 2 December); Nanaimo (4-9 December); and ends up with just two days in Vancouver. It is, all in all, a great success. He has vocabularies enough to complete a linguistic map of the B.C. coast; he has packed off enough museum specimens to pay for the trip; and his manuscript of myths and legends "has reached page 326" (Rohner, p. 73). The other three trips which furnished the stories of *Indianische Sagen* were at a similar pace. The British Association for the Advancement of Science instructed him, through Horatio Hale, not to attempt a thorough study of any one tribe but to compile a general synopsis, i.e. to continue the kind of rushing around he had proved he could do. He was

---

[3]For a full list of Boas's publications by year, including early pieces in German periodicals, see H.A. Andrews et al "Bibliography of Franz Boas," in the memorial volume of the *American Anthropologist* previously cited (1943) pp. 67-109.

[4]*The Ethnography of Franz Boas* ed. Ronald P. Rohner (University of Chicago Press 1969) p. 88. This work will be referred to many times, abbreviated as "Rohner." It is a compilation of Boas's family letters and diaries written on the Pacific Coast from 1886 to 1931, and is the full evidence for the summary Rohner presented in his article cited above (1966).

also asked to measure heads and collect skeletal remains, two disagreeable tasks which sapped his energies. It is a wonder that texts of permanent value could be obtained with so much scurrying. Perhaps Boas thought that few had, and left the collection untranslated, except for the following items which he placed in American journals:

(1) "On Certain Songs and Dances of the Kwakiutl of British Columbia" *Journal of American Folklore* 1 (1888) 49-64, which describes the potlatch Boas attended at Nawitti in 1886 and thus provides useful context (the materials appear in *Indianische Sagen* not so accommodated);

(2) "Notes on the Snanaimuq" *American Anthropologist* 2 (October 1899) 321-328 contains two tales from the Nanaimo section of *Indianische Sagen,* presented within the context of a description of tribal customs;

(3) "Salishan Texts" *Proceedings of the American Philosophical Society* 34 (January 1895) 31-48—Bella Coola texts with interlinear translation (the *Indianische Sagen* versions are longer, more sprawling, and may possibly be the same stories obtained through the medium of Chinook jargon);

(4) "Myths and Legends of the Catloltq [Comox] of Vancouver Island" *American Antiquarian* 10 (1888) 201-211, 366-373.

These are the selections from his earliest field work in myth that Boas offered his English-speaking public. Are they good stories? The question seems almost impertinent. Boas certainly would not claim that they were. Of the Bella Coola sampling, for instance, he states: "the texts are fragmentary and indifferent versions of myths" ("Salishan Texts" p. 31). In his letters home he makes it clear that he is really interested in the language: "The stories themselves are not worth much" (Rohner p. 50). When he says of the Comox stories, "in some ways the myths of the Comox are very interesting, and I am glad I have found so many of them" (Rohner p. 67), it is their pivotal position in the spread of motifs north to south along the coast which makes them interesting to him. The stories themselves are not especially interesting. And after a week at the Nawitti potlatch, Boas can write: "At present I am quite confused by the amount of nonsense to which I must listen" (Rohner p. 38). The tidbits that appear in "On Certain Songs and Dances of the Kwakiutl" are quite appetizing, but future readers of *Indianische Sagen* should be warned that they will not be spared page after page of what Boas himself was very puzzled by.

Boas in 1894

The 1894 season was surely Boas's best. It was his sixth, and he was lucky, and he had the skills to take advantage of his luck. As far as the British Association for the Advancement of Science was concerned, he was filling in gaps: the Nass River Tsimshian and the Tsetsaut. The ethnology is in his 1895 Report to the British Association; the myths and legends were published separately: "Traditions of the Tsetsaut" *Journal of American Folklore* 9 (1896) 257-268, and 10 (1897) 35-48; and *Tsimshian Texts* (Bureau of American Ethnology Bulletin 27, 1902). As far as his other sponsor was concerned, the U.S. National Museum wanted an article from him. He gave them much more, the magnificent *Social Organization and Secret Societies of the Kwakiutl,* published as pp. 311-738 of the Annual Report of the Smithsonian Institution for the Year Ending June 30, 1895 (Washington, D.C. 1897).

These results were achieved by Boas's willingness now to stick it out in a place until he gets a "break." When the S.S. Boskowitz arrived in Kinkolith on 10 October 1894, the Tsetsaut he was looking for were all away hunting. Boas sent for the old man of the tribe, with the promise that he would be well paid if he returned. Meanwhile, he busied himself with Tsimshian language and stories, and measuring the physique of the Indians who were available. He waited from 11 October to 24 October, when: "this afternoon, very unexpectedly, the old Tsetsaut appeared. You can imagine how happy I am. Now I can satisfactorily pursue the main work I had in mind for this place" (Rohner p. 163).

My first day with the Tsetsaut was a great disappointment. The man talks so terribly fast that I cannot get any proper material out of him. He may learn to speak more slowly if I insist on it, but I doubt it. I have to try my best, however. I worked the whole afternoon to learn the old habitat of the tribe and its relationship to the neighboring tribes. I am clear about it now, although it is a very slow process with him. He also gave me two legends and some linguistic material—vocabulary only (Rohner p. 164).

Well, Boas did persist; so that on 1 November he can say with some satisfaction: "It seems that I have learned everything my friend the Tsetsaut knows" (Rohner p. 168). Boas deserves a lot of points for his persistence, and it seems ungracious to take any of those points away from him. But why is his account of this informant, Levi, so uninteresting in his 1895 Report to the British Association, and why do Levi's stories in the *Journal of American Folklore* seem dull? We can be sure it wasn't Levi's fault. Rohner again gives us the spice. The letters have all the flavour which Boas denied his published reportage. Levi may have been "quite exasperating," but he wasn't boring:

> I ask him through my interpreter, "How do you say in Tsetsaut: 'If you don't come, the bear will run away'?" I could not get him to translate this. He would only say, "The Nass could be asked a thing like this; we Tsetsaut are always there when a bear is to be killed. That's why we can't say a thing like this" (Rohner p. 166).

This is the kind of thing Boas unfortunately considered unpublishable.

> I also asked him, "What is the name of the cave of the porcupine?" His answer was only, "A white

man could not find it anyway and therefore I don't have to tell you" (Rohner p. 166).

A man who can parry like that is not likely to tell stories as plain as the gruel of the *Journal of American Folklore* pieces attributed to him. Something has been lost in transmission.

Chief Mountain

Perhaps the best stories in *Tsimshian Texts* (1902), though lacking the interlinear translation that the others have, are those told by Chief Mountain, who, in the British Association Report (1895), is given a welcome modicum of biography:

> When he himself was a youth the supernatural beings were pursuing him all the time. One day a beautiful girl appeared to him and he fainted. She taught him her song which enabled him to make the olachen come in spring. . . . She wanted to have intercourse with him. One night she took him through a fire, and since that time he was able to handle fire with impunity. . . . At one time the Gyitqadeq disbelieved his power over fire. He asked them to build a large fire. He threw an iron hoop into it, moistened his hands, and covered his face, hair, and hands with eagle-down. Then he stepped barefooted over the glowing embers, took the redhot hoop, and carried it through the fire without burning his hands or his feet. He added that a few years ago he repeated this experiment, but as he failed and burnt his hands and feet he gave up his supernatural helper and became a Christian (pp. 580-581).

How refreshing that Boas does not turn this account into a disquisition on what shamans in general do. Mountain's personal authority must have been too great for him to be turned into a class of behaviour patterns.

It was in 1927, thirty-three years after Boas, that Marius Barbeau went to see Mountain:

His white hair reached down his shoulders, and he seemed blind, unable to sit up; after a while he could raise himself on an elbow. He was quite deaf. For a chief of his high standing, whose main crest was the Double-headed Eagle, like that of the Tzar's imperial emblem, there was certainly no mark here of power and prestige, and little promise that he might prove of much use in my research. . . . Once he was launched on to his narrative, we went smoothly ahead for a good part of the afternoon, he muttering a phrase or two, the interpreter conveying the meaning to me in English, and I recording in shorthand the story as it moved along without a hitch. But the old man slowly grew excited at the recital of the unforgotten trials of his ancestors; he raised himself on his elbows and his hands, shouting at times and singing. I feared that he might collapse, and die, perhaps. We adjourned until the next day, and found him expecting us. The revival of his tradition had brought cheer to him and perhaps a new span of life.[5]

Barbeau thus prepares us very nicely for "Origin of the Salmon-Eater Clan," given on pp. 16-21 of *Totem Poles* (Ottawa 1950) Vol. I, and for Mountain's explanation of his totem pole, the tallest in existence at that time. Barbeau gives us further insight into Mountain's character when he describes what Mountain replied to an offer to purchase his pole: "Give me the tombstone of Governor Douglas; I will give you the totem of my grand-uncles" (p. 33). Mountain died the following year, and when Barbeau came again, he bought the pole from his heirs, and it now stands in the Royal Ontario Museum in Toronto. He also picked up something else — a story about Mountain in his youth, deeply wounded in his pride because

---

[5]Marius Barbeau "Totems and Songs" *Canadian Geographical Journal* 50 (1955) 176-181, quotation p. 177.

his wife had left him for the favours of a Hudson's Bay official, Captain McNeill in Victoria:

> To wipe off his shame in good style among his people, Mountain waited for his opportunity in a big tribal feast in his village of Gitiks. There he held up in his hand ten beautiful marten skins, and sang to an old tune a new challenge which he had just composed to cast ridicule on the fair deserter. He sang with sarcasm: ". . . Wait and see what a chief can do! Wait, O sweetheart, that you may learn how, after my humiliation because of you, I have again raised my head! Wait, O flighty one, before you send me word of how you have failed in your foolish escapade and pine once more for my love! Time is now ripe, O woman who would rather belong to the bleached Victoria tribe (of white people) for you to send me a bottle of Old Tom. For my part I dispatch to you this small handful of mere beaver skins."
>
> Actually there was more than a "small handful," and the skins were even more valuable than beaver. They were picked marten such as an indignant and wealthy chief could sacrifice to heap ridicule upon a woman unworthy of him. She would surely, after her desertion, be unable to reciprocate in kind.

But she was able. The following year, through her brother, she met the challenge with a carved canoe.

> Now once more she had heaped humiliation upon him, and the tribe was not sure that he had the wit and the means to retaliate.
>
> He had. After all his wealth in pelts, copper shields, blankets and trade goods was gathered, he invited the neighbouring tribes and made it known that he was about to cast off his unfaithful wife in a way which would brand her forever as worthless. While he lavished presents upon his guests at a

feast, particularly upon those who had laughed at him, he sang a song composed for the occasion—a taunting song: "Hush! stop your idle chatter! Why do you mind my affairs?".... And the people had to repeat the refrain in chorus, after he had sung ....[6]

Mountain's ex-wife won in the end, for she erected the most fabulous of totem poles to the memory of her brother, confirming her status and freeing herself of Mountain's power (Barbeau got the pole in 1929!).

The point is that chiefs live their lives in public, and as storytellers they are also people about whom stories are told. Mountain was undoubtedly a high chief, and at the time Boas came on the scene was ruling his domains augustly. But we now have information on two failures in his life: his retirement as shaman, and his losing against his wife in a notorious "fight with property." We need not refrain, any more than his contemporaries would, from applying what we know. Here is Chief Mountain telling Boas about the origin of his own clan. The motif of the club which can turn whole towns into forest may be world-wide, but this is how Chief Mountain's version ends:

> The brothers travelled all over the world, and made war on all the tribes, and destroyed them by means of their club. The chief in heaven became angry because they abused his gift, and wished that they might forget the club on one of their expeditions. So it happened that they forgot the club when they

---

[6]Barbeau in the *Canadian Geographical Journal* article cited above, pp. 180-181. A recording was made later by Chief Tralarhaet (Frank Bolton), "a clan brother of Chief Mountain," also referred to as Geetiks, "the last of the pagans on the Nass"—see "Songs of the Northwest" *The Musical Quarterly* 19 (1933) p. 109; and "Tsimshian Songs," pp. 125-126 of *The Tsimshian, Their Arts and Music* (1951), where Barbeau transfers the authorship of the song and the story behind it, rather annoyingly, to someone else.

went out to attack the town Gulgeu. Therefore the place has been called ever since that time Hwildakstsax, or Where-the-club-was-forgotten. Then they went to Demlaxam on Skeena river, where they settled, as they were unable to continue fighting on account of the loss of the supernatural club. Their descendants became the Gisqahast.

If Boas had been present at a communal telling of this origin story, and had known what the audience knew about the storyteller, and had been on the lookout for nuances in tone, and had sought a means to communicate them, we would have had quite a different text before us, I believe. With heroic figures, the public and the private are the same thing; the tribal loss of a supernatural club is the symbolic equivalent of the storyteller's own.

The 1894 Fort Rupert Potlatch

In the introductory pages of *The Social Organization and the Secret Societies of the Kwakiutl Indians* (1897) Boas uses some of the material he obtained from Mountain, this time suppressing personal references, even his name. It is tedious to keep repeating how Boas's need to appear scientific deprives us of the individual quality of the event. This 1897 volume is very close to being the personal document we want of him; a whole section gives a play by play account of "The Winter Ceremonial at Fort Rupert" (pp. 544-606)—"the ceremonial as it actually took place and so far as I witnessed it in the winter of 1895-96."[7] But Boas is so successful in his scientific aim that he manages to tell us what he saw there as though he

[7]Though the letters edited by Rohner indicate that this date is obviously erroneous, and that Boas was in Fort Rupert from 14 November to 6 December 1894, Boas seems always to have referred to the potlatch as occurring in 1895. The manuscript in his posthumous papers, "The Winter Ceremonial at Fort Rupert, 1895," an almost verbatim copying of a section of the *Social Organization* volume, is printed by Helen Codere without correction of the date, in *Kwakiutl Ethnography* (University of Chicago Press 1966) pp. 179-241.

were the proverbial "camera," not a human observer. If we want to know how he felt, we have to turn again to the family letters (Rohner pp. 176-189). It would not have done any harm, even in a scholarly work, to indicate just how lucky he was to arrive, without precise expectation, at Fort Rupert in the middle of the winter dance season, and to see in the canoe that came to pick him up none other than George Hunt, whom he had met in 1888 in Victoria and who had been in Chicago for the World's Fair Exhibition in 1893. It would not have done any harm to take us behind the scenes a little. As the narrative stands in the *Social Organization* volume, it seems well nigh miraculous that he could have written down so much so promptly. We should have been made aware that Hunt was at his elbow at every event and filled in the details of speeches the next day, and that George Hunt's son, David, the chief of the Seal Society, a very influential Hamatsa, facilitated things in interesting ways. For instance, the very first potlatch Boas attended on his arrival, one that is not mentioned in the formal report, was obviously the most strategically important potlatch of them all:

> The first morning we discussed what I planned to do, and I invited all the Indians to a feast, which took place in the afternoon. That was a sight! There were about 250 Indians in the house—men, women and children. They were painted red and black, and wore jewelry; each was dressed in his cedar bark cloak. . . . Welcoming speeches were held for me and I was given the name Heiltsakuls, "the silent one." Then the master of ceremonies called the singers and told them what to sing. Every tribe—there were three tribes present—sang two songs, after which my "feast" came: hard tack and molasses. Before we ate I made my speech. I said that I had wanted to come for a long time and that I was glad to be here now. Then I spoke to the people who had been in Chicago and gave them their

pictures. . . . Next the Koskimo brought blankets and gave them away with appropriate speeches, telling the Kwakiutl that they were nice people and open-handed, etc. At the end he gave me a silver dollar, but I also had to make a speech, and of course I will have to give him $2 before I leave. The whole thing lasted four hours and cost me $14.50. Of course, I gained the good will of these people and received invitations to all the feasts which are taking place here (Rohner pp. 177-178).

So that's how it's done!

If only Boas could have fused the tidbits he was writing home with the serious business of his formal reports! In his letters he explains how the performers staged the striking of a woman's shoulder so that it looked like a very heavy blow: "The oar was, of course, very cleverly cut beforehand so that the onlookers thought it was really broken" (Rohner p. 185). In the *Social Organization and Secret Societies* volume, neither his tricks nor theirs get explained. There is only one joke in the whole book.[8] It is a very ponderous tome. I have called it "magnificent"—and it is, in its sheer quantity of description and illustration. It is more than magnificent; it is positively imperious. Boas does not bend to explain what's really going on. For the first time, myth and legend are placed in the midst of activity of which they are an essential part and from which insight should be derived. But Boas seems to assume we are following it all with interest and understanding, whereas we are really overfed with lumps of stuff we cannot digest. The raw materials are there; they are obviously authentic; the

---

[8]It is a joke which requires an explanation and doesn't get one. See *The Social Organization and the Secret Societies of the Kwakiutl* p. 546—equivalent to p. 180 in *Kwakiutl Ethnography* ed. Helen Codere (1966). Helen Codere also assumes we understand it when she deals with the "amiable" features of Boas's "1895-96" potlatch on p. 339 of her article, "The Amiable Side of Kwakiutl Life: The Potlatch and the Play Potlatch" *American Anthropologist* 58 (1956) 334-351.

mythology is attached to a sequence of ritualistic events that Boas witnessed and Hunt was able immediately to amplify. It is, in my opinion, Boas's highest achievement in field work on the Northwest Coast. But what are we going to do with it all?[9]

---

[9]Irving Goldman in *The Mouth of Heaven: An Introduction to Kwakiutl Religious Thought* (New York: John Wiley & Sons 1975) expresses his appreciation of this work of Boas's in particular (p. 12). He attempts a response to the religious and social aspects, and to the myth of the Man Eater (pp. 110-113), which is very interesting as far as it goes. Philip Drucker and Robert F. Heizer's *To Make My Name Good* (University of California 1967) is "a reexamination of the Southern Kwakiutl potlatch." The religious aspects, however, are neglected. In a recently published volume, *Feasting with Cannibals* (Princeton University Press 1981), Stanley Walens tries to rectify matters by searching Boas's Kwakiutl publications for metaphors of the spiritual life. He finds that the dominating image is that of eating. He draws on *The Social Organization and the Secret Societies of the Kwakiutl,* dealing with the 1894 potlatch as a distinctive event on pp. 138-163. We cannot here do justice to his interesting speculations.

Chapter IV
James Teit of Spences Bridge

Our first view of James Teit can be through the eyes of Dr. Snowden Dunn Scott, reporting on a meeting of B.C. Indian chiefs in Vancouver, probably around 1910:

> On a low chair by the table among the chiefs sat a silent white man, who took no part in the proceedings until the chiefs began to address the superintendent-general, each in his own language. Then he began to interpret. As one after another of the natives poured out his complaint or expressed his opinions in various forms of aboriginal eloquence, Mr. Teit in a low, quiet voice, rendered his appeal or argument into clear and cultured English. I was struck with the simplicity, felicity and clearness of his language. Every sentence was ready for the press.[1]

---

[1]Quoted by Judith Banks in her M.A. thesis *Comparative Biographies of Two British Columbia Anthropologists: Charles Hill-Tout and James A. Teit* (University of British Columbia 1970) p. 61, see also p. 202. Three of Teit's children contributed biographical reminiscences to Banks's thesis, which makes it the chief source for information on Teit's life.

It was a man of this authority, skill and bearing that Boas was to meet in 1894.

The family was "Tait" in the Shetlands, where James was born and raised; but it was as "Teit" that the young "Norseman" of eighteen or nineteen emigrated to Canada. He subsequently gave all his five children Scandinavian names. These were the children of his second marriage. His first marriage had been childless, but, in one sense, gave issue to all the works that bear his name. Little is known of Lucy Artko or Atello, who became Teit's wife in 1892 and died of pneumonia or tuberculosis in 1899, little except the significant fact that she was of the local tribe of Thompson Indians. Teit's life thus took a direction which made his meeting with Franz Boas almost inevitable.

Boas had had a bad night. He had arrived in Spences Bridge by train and, hammering at the hotel door, had been "offered a dirty bed shared with a drunken workman." "It was," he writes home on 21 September 1894, "worse than in an Indian house" (Rohner p. 139). (It was always one of Teit's advantages as an ethnographer that he had Indian houses to stay in, and so didn't have to use the B.C. local hotels.) Next morning someone told Boas about Teit, so he started the three-mile climb up the mountain trail. Teit, not knowing the fate that was approaching him, was out. Boas waited, "entertained by his wife and an old man," and after an hour Teit came. "The young man," Boas wrote home, "is a treasure! He knows a great deal about the tribes. I engaged him right away" (Rohner p. 139). Thus began a long and fruitful association.

There are two things to say in general about this association. One is that Boas edited and prepared for publication all of Teit's work printed in his lifetime, so that it is impossible to entirely separate the pupil's contribution from the teacher's. On the other hand, we do have a way of easily distinguishing a Teit story from a Boas story: we are invariably struck, as Dr. Snowden Dunn Scott was, by the simplicity, felicity, and clearness of Teit's language.

Unfortunately, however, we know that Native tales do not

"Jimmy Teit and a Rocky Mountain Goat"—illustration in Frantz Rosenberg's *Big Game Shooting in British Columbia and Norway* (London: Martin Hopkinson 1928).

really get told in clear and cultured sentences that are ready for the press. And if we state that Teit's first collection, published as Vol. 6 of the Memoirs of the American Folk-Lore Society, entitled *Traditions of the Thompson River Indians of British Columbia* (1898), is almost flawless, the adjective is double-edged. We might wish that more of the natural flaws of the original performances would show. Teit provides us with two or three literal interlinear translations in his notes, so that we can see what he does with them for his elegant free translations. The Mosquito legend is a crucial test case. I give the literal translation first:

His Myth the Mosquito and the Thunder

Arrived when had improved the earth, then departed the mosquito to people, then he stayed there. He stayed there with the people; then he heard his voice the Thunder. He said the Thunder "Some time shall I kill them the people." Being then the mosquito he bites from the bodies of the people; he sucked the blood, therefore immensely swollen his body. Then he departed to his house the Thunder. He arrived at the Thunder his house; then he said to him the mosquito he asked him: "Why thou fat, if whence thou that therefore much thy food." Then said the mosquito: "Shall I tell thee, thou do say that wilt thou kill them the people, thou do long for them." He went he pointed out to him therefore to tree the its top. "From the trees when I eat it, that them whom thou killest them, because that fat, fat because that therefore we are fat when thou seest us." Then he said the Thunder: "I think really thou liest, not they people the trees, not they have blood, yet then it is the much blood in ye." Then said the mosquito: "Not I lie, from tree that when we obtain it the its blood the tree that our food." Then said the Thunder: "Enough! well that shall I kill, sometimes if I see fit, then I kill it the tree." Perhaps he told the mosquito, surely then he treated them the people as he treats them the trees. He pitied them the people the mosquito. Then not he told him (p. 111).

The story in the body of the text on p. 56 is the version Teit wants to serve to us on proper china ware:

The Mosquito and the Thunder
(Nkamtcinemux)

Once the Mosquito paid a visit to the Thunder. The latter, seeing that the Mosquito was gorged with blood, asked him where he obtained it, and told him that he had been wishing to get some for a long time, but did not know where to obtain it. The Mosquito answered, "I got the blood from somewhere." The Thunder was annoyed at this evasive answer, and said, "Why do you answer me thus? Don't you know that I can shoot you and kill you?" The Mosquito, being afraid, then said, "I suck it from the tree-tops." By this lie the Mosquito saved the people, and that is the reason that the Thunder strikes the tree-tops at the present-day. If the Mosquito had told the truth, then the Thunder would now shoot people and animals instead of trees.

The felicity of this free version is immediately obvious; but what about its fidelity to the original text? Rather unsatisfactory. Mosquito, in the original, at no time acts from evasiveness or fear but, on hearing what Thunder threatens to do to the people, embarks on a deliberate strategy of deceit to deflect Thunder from the people on to the trees. Thunder's blustering is either something that Teit himself added for dramatic effect or it came from another telling of the same story; probably the latter, since Teit's stories are sometimes composites. In any case, the discrepancy between what is offered as the literal "Indian" version on p. 111 and the free version on p.

56 makes one uneasy. The other two interlinear examples in the volume match their free version quite well; but the mosquito legend we have just examined shows what leaps Teit is capable of.

And just to see where this kind of rewriting gets one, we can turn to the Abstracts of the stories, provided by Boas at the back of the volume:

The Mosquito and the Thunder

When the Thunder desired to eat blood, the Mosquito told him that he obtained it from the tops of trees. For this reason the Thunder strikes the tree-tops (p. 127).

This, it seems to me, is getting hold of just the wrong end of the stick. The original narrative is not answering the question: "Why does thunder strike tree-tops?" but rather is meeting a desire to adjust to the presence of mosquitoes in the world. The Native storyteller is saying: "The mosquito is a nuisance, but in the early time he saved us from Thunder." Boas's abstract is etiological, as is Teit's blue-plate version. Ask why the elephant has a long trunk, and you will get a "Just-so" story, a fanciful fiction of how something came to be. But Malinowski long ago asserted that primitive man does not ask such questions.[2] If Teit came across Natives who did, then it's probably because a Kipling, or a missionary, or a Teit has had

---

[2]Bronislaw Malinowski "Myth in Primitive Psychology" (1926) included in *Magic, Science and Religion* (Anchor Books 1954). Teit must have been looking out for etiological aspects of legends when he went collecting at Telegraph Creek and Dease Lake in 1915. The Tahltan and Kaska seemed to require that everything be explained, and in italics. Even the dog-children story, which can be very moving in some renderings, is bent to explain why *marmots are scarce on the north side of the Stikine River*—"Tahltan Tales" *Journal of American Folklore* 32 (1919) 198-250 and 34 (1921) 223-253, quotation on p. 250. The same story told by the same people in 1903 exhibited no such passion to explain the scarcity of marmots—see Teit's "Two Tahltan Traditions" *Journal of American Folklore* 22 (1909) 314-318.

an influence. There is an enormous difference between (a) a Mosquito who tricks Thunder into striking tree-tops instead of people, and (b) a Mosquito who is alert to Thunder's propensities and has enough feeling for people to want to save them by serious subterfuge. The first is cute; the second provides a grounding for moral structure. Mosquitoes are a real threat to anybody's concept of a benificent world. The Thompson Indians have a story to take care of the annoyance, and possibly deeper questions. The story says it could be a lot worse: but for the mosquito, it could be Thunder after our blood.

Under the title of this story Teit gives a tribal name. He was presumably asked to locate his stories geographically in this way, and he does so throughout his work. The idea must be that we might be able to say something precise about distribution of themes. But this, to my mind, merely leads to another major error. The Transformer brothers story pp. 42-45 in *Traditions of the Thompson River Indians* provides a case in point:

> Once when the Coyote was away from home, the Qoaqlqal [Transformer Brothers] passed by his house, and, finding his wife there alone, they threw her into the fire of the lodge, where she was consumed (p. 44).

They repair the damage by giving Coyote two other wives, but their behaviour seems nothing short of criminally mischievous. The location of this story is given as Nkamtcinemux, from which we conclude that for the Upper Thompson Indians the Transformer tales do not, in the words of Boas's Introduction (p. 11), "by any means bring out an altruistic point of view." But wait. In Teit's *Mythology of the Thompson Indians* (1912) we find a rather different version of the same episode:

> Continuing their travels up the river, the brothers came to another underground house, which they entered. This house was also inhabited by Coyote, who happened to be away at the time, gathering

firewood. The brothers sat down inside; but, as the weather was rather chilly, they presently wished to have a fire. They looked in vain for any fire-wood in the lodge, but at last discovered a piece of wood with a knot-hole in it, which was covered over with a lot of robes. They split it up and made a fire with it. This piece of wood was Coyote's wife (p. 222).

Now, this story is attributed to the Fraser Canyon Thompson. So what should we deduce from the different versions in the different locations? That for the Upper Thompson River Indians the Transformer brothers were callous people who might casually burn someone's wife, whereas for the Fraser Canyon Indians the brothers are just a little chilly and need a fire? This would be an absurd deduction. What really happened is that in 1898 Boas and Teit published a rather feeble version of the knot-hole wife story, so badly told that it led them astray. One is amazed that they did not even at that time know any better, but this is not the point. By always putting the tribal name as a subheading to the stories, they perpetuate the notion that variations in stories are attributable to dispersion, whereas it seems to be only common sense that variations will be due, in large part, to whether or not you are listening to a good storyteller.

Furthermore, the repetition of phrases like "the Shuswap have a version" or "see the Lower Thompson version" fosters a habit of mind where the individual informant is assumed to be merely a vehicle for tribal lore. This assumption allows Boas to discuss tribal characteristics and diffusion of myths on the basis of very few particulars, perhaps only a single testimony. When Boas in his reports says "according to my information," we tend to think he has numerous samples for his empirical conclusions, whereas the likelihood is that he didn't. In his "Mythology and Folk-Tales of the North American Indians" *Journal of American Folklore* 27 (1914) pp. 374-410, reprinted in his *Race, Language and Culture* (1940), Boas makes this general statement:

> Perhaps the most characteristic feature of these culture-hero tales is their lack of detail. Many are bare statements of the fact that something was different from the way it is now. The hero performs some very simple act, and ordains that these conditions shall be changed. It is only when the culture-hero concept rises to greater heights, as it does in the South, that these tales acquire greater complexity (p. 474).

Admittedly, in the worst tellings, these Transformer stories read just like one old transformed rock after another. But we might have said the same thing about Ovid's *Metamorphoses,* if Ovid had not been a better writer than his imitators. Go out on Harrison Lake and ignore certain rocks and see what wind will come up to overturn your canoe! These rock stories have a practical importance, which is attached to the imaginative life of the local people. But there are not too many Ovids around; and if you are paying just anybody to tell you stories, you are going to get quite a lot of "bare statements." I do not know what tribes Boas had in mind from the South to give them preeminence in this matter; but as far as the Northwest is concerned, he was reviewing a corpus which included many inadequately told stories. Unfortunately Teit supplied him with quite a few of them.

One further illustration on this point. In a much-told story Coyote becomes lustful for one of his son's wives. The question is why one rather than the other. In the *Traditions* volume (1898) we find:

> Coyote took advantage of an opportunity to examine the women, in order to determine which would please him best. He was not favorably impressed with the dark-skinned one but took a fancy to her fairer sister (p. 24).

A footnote number sends one to the back of the book: "The full version of this passage is as follows: *Canis occasione oblata, sub vestimenta mulierum pudenda suspexit.*" So much for the Victorian nineteenth century. I don't know whether it was Teit or Boas who decided to translate these bits into Latin so that only clergymen could read them, but there they are. By the time of the *Mythology of the Thompson* of 1912, we can have it in English:

> Coyote was jealous of his son's wives, and coveted them for himself. He did not know, however, which of them he liked the better: so one night he made a very large fire, and, taking advantage of the bright blaze, he watched his chance to look at the women's privates. He was so favorably impressed with those of the fair one that he at once made up his mind to get rid of his son, and take possession of his wife for himself (p. 205).

That this is not in Latin makes it, if anything, less interesting. What *really* happened was that, acting on a flicker of lust, Coyote went and asked the different trees whether or not they made a lot of sparks as they burned. Cedar said he made the most, so Coyote built up a fire of cedar, and the sparks really flew. One of his son's wives was an eagle-wife, and she drew back from the fire so that her dress would not be scorched. The duck-wife, on the other hand, was too lazy to move, and just pulled her knees up to her chest. Now, that's more interesting. And it's more interesting not because of the tribe from which it comes (because actually it's from the same Thompson tribe), but because the man who told it with just the right edge to it was rather a brilliant storyteller named Chief Mischelle of Lytton.[3]

The fact that stories from obvious European sources are told by the Indians raises the question of dispersion in a most

---

[3] *The Salish People* (1978) Vol. I p. 89. Chief Mischelle's version of the Transformer Story, which Hill-Tout collected in 1896, is very full and detailed: see *The Salish People* (1978) Vol. I pp. 32-34. It is the epic against which the various "collapsed" versions can be measured.

direct way. *Mythology of the Thompson Indians* (1912) had a section of "Tales Based on European Folklore"; and Teit published a further selection, "European Tales from the Upper Thompson Indians" in *Journal of American Folklore* 29 (1916) 301-329, where Boas supplied notes. Unfortunately his references are mainly to a German book of *Hausmärchen,* and I am not aware of any study that is very helpful in explaining the intrusion of these old folk tales into the Northwest. Boas has a short piece, "Romance Folk-lore Among American Indians," collected in *Race, Language and Culture* (1940) pp. 517-524; but even the more plausible remarks are suspect. "Fairy tales like the story of Seven-Heads and John the Bear are found wherever the French fur-trader went" (p. 517). All right, but when Teit is collecting tales from the Kaska of Dease Lake in 1915 he makes a point of inquiring for "such tales as those of Petit Jean, John the Bear, and others, but without result."[4] Tales of European origin appear to be altogether unknown there. Are we therefore to assume that French fur-traders never got as far as Dease Lake? The question of dispersion is, in any case, much less interesting than that of the status of these European stories in the repertoire of the Indian narrator. Were they told on certain social occasions? With mockery? With acknowledgment of the alien elements, or as part of the Native oral tradition of the area? The Petit John stories, Teit says in his "European Tales" article, "have been told in the tribe at least for sixty or seventy years; how much longer is difficult to say. Some people considered them to be white man's stories, although they could not state how they came to be told by the Indians" (p. 313). This statement is quite vague, but it's all we get on the subject.[5]

---

[4]James Teit "Kaska Tales" *Journal of American Folklore* 30 (1917) 427-473, quotation p. 429.

[5]Lucy Kramer, the editor of Teit's posthumous "More Thompson Indian Tales" *Journal of American Folklore* 50 (1937) 173-190, includes further "stories of European provenience" (pp. 177-190) and in a footnote on pp. 184-185 quotes a Teit letter to Boas, where he feels that the stories came prior to 1830 along "the main trade

We can complete our review of the stories Teit collected from the people he lived amongst by turning briefly to the "Thompson Tales" section of *Folk-Tales of Salishan and Sahaptin Tribes* (1917). Perhaps the only question to ask is why, after the forty-eight stories in *Traditions of the Thompson River Indians* (1898), the 167 stories of *Mythology of the Thompson Indians* (1912), and the sixteen "European Tales from the Upper Thompson" (1916), one would want to add forty more, when they are quite undistinguished. Chief Tetlenitsa, who was in Ottawa with Teit in 1912, presenting a petition on the land question,[6] tells some of them, and it is interesting to see what he tells, even if his memory is a little rusty. But all in all the stories tend to the short and fragmentary; some are mere summaries:

> In La Fontaine they burned Coyote's wooden wife, and made two wives for him out of cottonwood and alder trees, and blew breath into them, thus transforming them into people (p. 19).

---

and cultural route" from the southeast through the Sahaptin and Shoshonean tribes. Nothing is quoted on the attitude of his informants to these peculiar imports. A general discussion of acculturation in respect to borrowed folk tales is to be found in Alan Dundes *The Morphology of North American Indian Folktales* (Helsinki 1964) Ch. VI: "It is virtually a platitude among folklorists that borrowed tales may often be adapted to fit the borrower's local folktale patterns. However, there have been almost no studies showing the details of such adaptation" (p. 99). See also Stith Thompson *European Tales Among the North American Indians* (Colorado Springs 1919), and Chapter VIII of his *Tales of the North American Indians* (Indiana University Press 1929). A 1957 commentary on a tribe visited by Teit in the early 1900's is particularly pertinent: Bruce B. MacLachlan "Notes on Some Tahltan Oral Literature" *Anthropologica* 4 (1957) 1-9. Jarold Ramsey uses Teit material to discuss a particular aspect of European influence in his "The Bible in Western Indian Mythology" *Journal of American Folklore* 90 (1977) 442-454.

[6]"Indian Chiefs Discuss the Land Question With Premier Borden," a clipping from the Vancouver *Province* (17 February 1912), in Vancouver City Archives.

"Blew breath into them" adds a Biblical flavour to this very "collapsed" telling of a familiar episode. Teit was surely not presenting it as good storytelling, but as possible further evidence for some proposition in myth scholarship. A footnote on p. 63 suggests this when it says: "I include the story here because of some similarity to an incident in a Shoshoni myth." This is really Boas speaking, or Teit as a Boas pupil.

Hence, the problem. What Teit was asked to do he did superbly well. But why doesn't he tell us something about his informants? He's more concerned that we should know who made baskets than who told stories.[7] And when he does tell us, as he does in *The Shuswap* (Jesup 1909), naming the two men who gave him fifty-two and twelve myths, respectively, and even allowing the first of these a fine two-page introduction (pp. 621-622), how come nothing of the personalities of these two men seems to get into the stories? How come the last twelve sound just like the first fifty-two? There is probably a very simple answer to these complaints: Teit did not take that kind of care over his myths because, simply, it was not asked for.

Let us be more positive and see where Teit is at his best. For all the reservations previously stated, Teit's first book, *Traditions of the Thompson River Indians* (1898), is excellent. After this tour de force, one can jump to the "Okanagan Tales" in *Folk-Tales of Salishan and Sahaptin Tribes,* edited by Boas as Vol. 11 of the Memoirs of the American Folklore Society (1917) pp. 65-92. Kwelweltaxen (Red-Arm), who told practically all these stories, was a real find. His repertoire is not extensive, but everything he tells has a twinkle to it. For instance, his Origin Myth includes the Garden of Eden and

---

Teit is very attentive to his informants in "Coiled Basketry in British Columbia and Surrounding Region," edited by Boas for the *Forty-First Annual Report of the Bureau of Ethnology* (Washington 1928), especially pp. 431-462. "Mr. Teit collected from the numbered informants with whom he worked so long quite complete data regarding themselves and their individual achievements, from which some very interesting deductions may be obtained about the different abilities and general intelligence of the women" (p. 431).

Jesus Christ; but Jesus is something of a failure: "He taught them no arts, nor wisdom about how to do things, nor did he help to make life easier for them. Neither did he transform or destroy the evil monsters which killed them, nor did he change or arrange the features of the earth in any way." Coyote was sent down by the Chief to rectify these deficiencies (pp. 81-82).

Teit's most attractive collection is "Traditions of the Lillooet Indians of British Columbia" *Journal of American Folklore* 25 (1912) 287-371, but it is hard to say why.[8] Perhaps it is that I come to it after being impressed by Hill-Tout's Lillooet collection, in *The Salish People* Vol. 2; and by *Lillooet Stories* edited by Randy Bouchard and Dorothy I.D. Kennedy for *Sound Heritage* Vol. 6 (1977), with the cassette of Charlie Mack and Baptiste Ritchie performing some of the stories; and by William Elliott's "Lake Lillooet Tales" *Journal of American Folklore* 44 (1931) 166-181. There may be a kind of self-deception operating here, as in what often passes for literary judgment. It is not surprising that one likes what one is *prepared* to like. One likes Teit's Lillooet better than his Shuswap, say, simply because one is already a Lillooet fan? Ah, but maybe one is a Lillooet fan because the Lillooet are good storytellers, and Teit's collection just confirms that fact? Objectivity is a bit of a will-o'-the-wisp; it is usually a matter of finding reasonable arguments for what one has stumbled into liking.

We should not leave Teit without looking back at the view of him we started with. He was a political advisor to the Indians of B.C., a translator of their petitions and advocate of their aspirations. He was the secretary of the Allied Tribes of B.C. organization.[9] Who, however, from reading his ethnographic reports, would gain an inkling of the depth of his

---

[8]Tristram P. Coffin chose two tales from this collection for his *Indian Tales of North America* (Philadelphia: American Folklore Society 1961).

[9]Philip Drucker *The Native Brotherhoods* (Bureau of American Ethnology Bulletin 168, 1958) pp. 95 and 98.

social mission? Boas knew about it; his obituary of Teit in the *Journal of American Folklore* 36 (1923) 102-103 spoke of it:

> While he was carrying on all these researches he became more and more interested in the difficulties against which the Indians have to contend, and his warm sympathy for their suffering led him to undertake the organization of the Indian tribes into an association for the protection of their rights . . . . Unceasingly he labored for their welfare and subordinated all other interests, scientific as well as personal, to this work, which he came to consider the most important task of his life (p. 103).

Boas knew about it all along; but as his mentor and editor he seems to have had no inclination to help Teit unify his two passions, ethnographic research and Native rights. They stayed separate. What Teit really knew about the Indians, their inner life and aspirations and how their politics connected to their tribal past, will never be published. It was never written down. It was not asked for.

Chapter V
Franz Boas: Collaborations

John Comfort Fillmore, Ethnomusicologist

As Boas's collaborator on *The Social Organization and the Secret Societies of the Kwakiutl* (1897), Hunt has his name on the title page: "Based on Personal Observations and on Notes Made by Mr. George Hunt." Before we turn to Hunt, we should look briefly at someone else who had a hand in the volume, specifically the songs to be found in the appendix. John Comfort Fillmore was a professor of music who had worked with Alice Fletcher on Omaha songs and had gone to the Chicago World's Fair to listen to the Kwakiutl whom Boas had brought there:

> Close at my right knee sat Duquayis, chieftainess of the tribe, a bright-looking, cheerful, responsive young woman of about twenty-two years of age. She was nursing her baby, a strong healthy-looking child. On the other side of me sat another young woman, whom she had called to sing with her a woman's song of the tribe, for my especial benefit.

We are grateful to Boas for publishing Fillmore's description in the *Journal of American Folklore,* even though it is the kind of writing he never found himself able to do:

> At first they were evidently a little abashed. They
> began at a low pitch, sang quite softly, and the
> intonation of the lowest tone was somewhat uncer-
> tain. I noted down the song as fast as I could; but, as
> they sang faster than I could write, I soon had to ask
> them to repeat a portion of it. Then I sang it with
> them, which seemed to afford them a good deal of
> amusement. . . . I smiled and laughed good-natured-
> ly with them and sang away with as much assurance
> as if I had felt myself competent to take Alvary's
> place in "Siegfried." Considering how short the
> song is, it required a good deal of time to get it
> down.[1]

Fillmore subsequently used phonographic cylinders, and
transcribed a number of songs. Boas took Fillmore's versions
with him to Fort Rupert the following year and was able to
compare them with the songs as sung by the Indians there:

> Today I corrected a few of the songs Fillmore
> wrote down in Chicago. Either the Indians sang
> very differently into the phonograph, or he could
> not hear them well. I am positive that I have written
> them down correctly now, and the difference
> between my rendering and his is immense (family
> letter 17 November 1894, Rohner p. 179).

---

[1]John Comfort Fillmore "A Woman's Song of the Kwakiutl
Indians" *Journal of American Folklore* 6 (1893) 285-291, quotations
from pp. 285-6. Fillmore's introduction to what becomes a rather
technical discussion of musical characteristics gives us a further
glimpse of James Deans: "the old Scotchman who represented the
British government there and had been interpreting for me, turned
to me and said, very impressively: 'You must know, sir, that Duquayis
has just done you the greatest honor in her power. She has not only
given you a woman's song; she has given you her own particular
song,—the song of the chieftainess, which she alone sings at the
potlatch'" (p. 286).

These reservations about Fillmore's work were not expressed in the *Social Organization* volume nor in the small collection of "Songs of the Kwakiutl Indians" published in 1896, where Boas—quite amazingly—is able to say: "On the whole our renderings of the music agree closely."[2]

With the case of Fillmore, then, we are raising a question about Boas's collaborations that we will have to raise several times in this chapter. What are we to think when Boas publishes the work of others under his own imprimatur without critical evaluation, without sharing with his readers some of the doubts we suspect, and sometimes know, he had?

The Jesup Expedition

George Hunt's work was financed for several years under the auspices of the Jesup North Pacific Expedition; we get our best introduction to his unique contribution to myth-collecting by looking at him in the context of this major group enterprise. Dr. Morris K. Jesup was the President of the American Museum of Natural History in New York when Boas was hired as Assistant Curator to F.W. Putnam in 1896. Boas convinced him that a massive research effort on both sides of the Bering Strait would answer questions about the migration of populations into North America and the origin of the coastal Indian tribes. The following list of the volumes ultimately published in the Jesup series (reprinted by AMS in 1975) indicates the range of Boas's conception:

Vol. 1. Pt. 1. Boas, F., *Facial Paintings of the Indians of Northern British Columbia.* New York, 1898.

Vol. 1. Pt. 2. Boas, F. *The Mythology of the Bella Coola Indians.* New York, 1898.

Vol. 1. Pt. 3. Smith, H.I., *Archaeology of Lytton, British Columbia.* New York, 1899.

---

[2]Franz Boas "Songs of the Kwakiutl Indians" *Internationales Archiv für Ethnographie* 9 (1896) Supplement pp. 1-9, quotation on p. 1.

Vol. 1. Pt. 4. Teit, J.A., *The Thompson Indians of British Columbia.* New York, 1900.

Vol. 1. Pt. 5. Farrand, L., *Basketry Designs of the Salish Indians.* New York, 1900.

Vol. 1. Pt. 6. Smith, H.I., *Archaeology of the Thompson River Region, British Columbia.* Includes Index to Vol. 1, Pts. 1-6. New York, 1900.

Vol. 2. Pt. 1. Farrand, L., *Traditions of the Chilcotin Indians.* New York, 1900.

Vol. 2. Pt. 2. Smith, H.I. and G. Fowke, *Cairns of British Columbia and Washington.* New York, 1901.

Vol. 2. Pt. 3. Farrand, L. and W.S. Kahnweiler, *Traditions of the Quinault Indians.* New York, 1902.

Vol. 2. Pt. 4. Smith, H.I., *Shell-Heaps of the Lower Fraser River, British Columbia.* New York, 1903.

Vol. 2. Pt. 5. Teit, J.A., *The Lillooet Indians.* Leiden and New York, 1906.

Vol. 2. Pt. 6. Smith, H.I., *Archaeology of the Gulf of Georgia and Puget Sound.* Leiden and New York, 1907.

Vol. 2. Pt. 7. Teit, J.A., *The Shuswap.* Includes Index to Vol. 2, Pts. 1-7. Leiden and New York, 1909.

Vol. 3. Boas, F. and G. Hunt, *Kwakiutl Texts.* Leiden and New York, 1905.

Vol. 4. Laufer, B., *The Decorative Art of the Amur Tribes.* New York, 1902.

Vol. 5. Pt. 1. Swanton, J.R., *Contributions to the Ethnology of the Haida.* Leiden and New York, 1905.

Vol. 5. Pt. 2. Boas, F., *The Kwakiutl of Vancouver Island.* Leiden and New York, 1909.

Vol. 6. Iokhél'son, V.I., *The Koryak.* Leiden and New York, 1905-1908.

Vol. 7. Bogoraz, V.G., *The Chukchee.* Leiden and New York, 1904-1909.

Vol. 8. Pt. 1. Bogoraz, V.G., *Chukchee Mythology.* Leiden and New York, 1910.

Vol. 8. Pt. 2. Teit, J.A., *Mythology of the Thompson Indians.* Leiden and New York, 1912.

Vol. 8. Pt. 3. Bogoraz, V.G., *The Eskimo of Siberia.* Leiden and New York, 1913.

Vol. 9. Iokhél'son, V.I., *The Yukaghir and the Yukaghirized Tungus.* Leiden and New York, 1926.

Vol. 10. Pt. 1. Boas, F. and G. Hunt, *Kwakiutl Texts—Second Series.* Leiden and New York, 1906.

Vol. 10. Pt. 2. Swanton, J.R., *Haida Texts—Masset Dialect.* Leiden and New York, 1908.

Vol. 11. Oetteking, B. *Craniology of the North Pacific Coast.* Leiden and New York, 1930.

Jesup North Pacific Expedition, *Ethnographical Album of the North Pacific Coasts of America and Asia.* New York, 1900.

By consulting the *Memoirs of the American Museum of Natural History* Vol. 2 dated 16 June 1898 pp. 3-12, one obtains in a few pages Boas's account of the "Operations of the Expedition in 1897." But, again, it is from the family letters, beginning on page 201 of Rohner, that we get the feeling of the thing, the exuberance of the setting forth of Boas, Livingston Farrand, and the archaeologist Harlan I. Smith, the regular triumvirate of the Expedition in its first year. Because of the good impression James Teit had made in 1894, Spences Bridge was the first stop; and their optimism increased. On June 5 Boas writes home: "If it will only continue this way! We have measured ten people and have photographed them, and I bought a small collection of ethnographic artifacts" (Rohner p. 202). Teit had prepared everything very well. While Farrand and Smith got the plaster casts of the Indians ready for shipping, he and Boas took the phonograph down to the village and recorded ten good songs:

> While they sang they acted out all their old stories and ceremonies. An old woman sang the song into the phonograph which serves to "cleanse" women who had borne twins. She took bundles of fir branches and hit her shoulders and breasts with them while she danced. The song imitates the growl of the grizzly bear because they believe that the children derive from the grizzly bear. An old man sang an old religious song to the sun, a prayer. The gestures were very expressive. He raised his hands up high and looked at the sun. Then he lowered them slowly, pressing them against his chest while he looked down again. The singing was a great deal of fun for the villagers. Some of the people were bashful, especially the women, who did not want to sing until all the men had left the house (Rohner pp. 203-204, letter dated 6 June 1897).

This seems like an exciting occasion. Some day the phonograph cylinders will be transcribed, and the event made available to us. The Jesup Expedition volumes seem unable to have found a place to mention it.

Livingston Farrand

Boas and Farrand, accompanied by Teit (Smith was left behind to do archaeological digs in Kamloops), began their trek across the rugged Chilcotin country with "four riding horses, five pack horses, and three guides" (Rohner p. 205). When there is ethnographic work to do, Boas and Farrand stay behind, and catch up with the party later. Farrand is a compatible companion, "unassuming and gay" (Rohner p. 206). There is no time to talk during the day, but the evenings are always agreeable. However, in order that the trip might be more advantageous to Farrand professionally, Boas reluctantly decides that Farrand should have a month alone in the Chilcotin. The stories that Farrand collected in these intensive weeks of independent work appear as Vol. 2 part 1 of the Jesup Publication, *Traditions of the Chilcotin Indians* (1900).

Farrand writes a modest and helpful introduction, mulling over problems of dispersal of myth-themes, and provides notes on "comparison with the mythologies of other tribes, which is, after all, the great object of the work" (p. 4). He is under Boas's direction here; but in one particular case he does help us see the human side of "dissemination," in giving the history of "The Story of Waiwailus":

> When this tale was first told the writer, it was recognized as being almost word for word the Bella Coola story of "Wawalis." Inquiry of the narrator as to where it had first been heard only brought out the assurance that it had always been known in the tribe, and was one of their oldest traditions. Repeated inquiries of different individuals elicited the same assertion; but finally certain of the older Indians agreed that they had first heard the tale in their younger days from a man who, though very old, was fortunately still living at the time of the writer's visit. When this old man was questioned, he immediately answered without hesitation, that when a child he had been captured by the Bella Coola, and had lived with them for several years before being restored to his tribe, and that during his captivity he had heard the story, and had brought it to his people on his return (p. 6).

This anecdote makes it easier to understand the reality behind "dispersion" of myths.

Farrand is a neat and thorough person, and his work reflects it, the thirty-two tales in this collection being far too well-mannered to be very close to the originals. They are, it is clear, "committee" stories: "All the tales recorded were checked by frequent repetition, and by independent narration from as many individuals as possible" (p. 4). Farrand had been educated at Princeton, and gained his M.D. from the College of Physicians and Surgeons. He had studied at Cambridge, England, in 1891, and at Berlin in 1892, and had returned to Columbia University in 1893 to teach in the Department of Psychology. His interest in Anthropology led him into contact with his fellow faculty member, Boas, and his mastery of German no doubt added to his impeccable qualifications. He did a surprising amount of work in a short time. After the Chilcotin weeks he spent the rest of the 1897 season with the Bella Bella at Rivers Inlet. His "Myths of the Bella Bella" was included in *Tsimshian Mythology* (1916) pp. 883-888, heavily edited by Boas. In 1898 he was on the Washington Coast for the Jesup Expedition, and his *Traditions of the Quinault Indians* was published in the series (1902). His "Quileute Tales" were presumably gathered at the same time, though edited somewhat later by Teresa Mayer for *Journal of American Folklore* 32 (1919) 251-279. He was in Oregon in 1900 and in Washington again in 1902; but not long after that he moved on to other concerns, and the field work was left to others to edit. He was important in the national campaign against tuberculosis. He was President of Cornell University for sixteen years. When he died in 1939 his fame belonged to the larger world, and his obituaries were not written in anthropological journals.[3]

Bella Coola

The last leg of the arduous five weeks' journey was the dramatic descent of 5,000 feet into Bella Coola itself. Boas gives himself space in his letters to paint the picture:

> The view was gorgeous. There were steep moun-
> taintops with huge glaciers, and in the valley a sea

---

[3]Information from obituary in *New York Times* 9 November 1939 p. 23.

of clouds through which one could see the river. The landscape was magnificent. We caught a marmot which served us as dinner. If I had the time and the desire, there would be plenty of opportunity to hunt. There are hundreds of fresh tracks of elk, black bears, and grizzly bears. Our guide shot at a grizzly bear, but he got away (Rohner p. 214).

At the end, Boas rode on ahead of the others because he had written to George Hunt when to expect him, and he did not want to pass the set date. Hunt was waiting as planned, and had everything well prepared. Teit let the horses rest for two days, then started back, with greetings for Farrand, should he meet him on the way. Boas then began work in earnest, "going over all the old Kwakiutl manuscripts with Hunt" (Rohner p. 215, letter of 23 July 1897).

Before we try to review that Kwakiutl work, we might glance at the Bella Coola work that Boas was doing at the same time. He wants to test his previous Bella Coola findings; but his informant, who seems to be a good one, has a weakness: he can't resist topping everything that Boas learned previously. Boas cross-examines him thoroughly, and on 30 July 1897 writes: "Thus far I have found him very reliable" (Rohner p. 216). By 3 August 1897 the informant is "completely squeezed dry"; the steamer is arriving the next day, and Boas is "quite satisfied with the results" (Rohner p. 217). The results were published in the Jesup series as *The Mythology of the Bella Coola Indians* (1898).

The informant is not even referred to in the volume, presumably because Boas wishes to have the freedom to refer to his findings as belonging to the Bella Coola as a whole. Yet, at the same time, he is quite aware that individual Bella Coola families have their own versions of myths, inconsistent with other family versions, even in regard to important events in the origin of the tribe:

> Some families maintain that the Raven liberated
> the sun, while, according to another one, the Mink

was essential in bringing about the present state of affairs. Still others say that Totosonx, during his travels, caused the sun to appear. The discrepancies in the traditions referring to the visit of the Mink and Wasp to their father, the Sun, are also very remarkable. Although a considerable amount of contradiction is inherent in all the mythologies of the North Pacific coast, they nowhere reach such a degree as among the Bella Coola; and I presume the fact that the traditions are kept secret by the various families accounts for this curious condition (pp. 125-126).

Thus Boas at the end of his book. But at the beginning he is ready to present his one informant's account of the five-fold heaven of the Bella Coola as gospel. T.F. McIlwraith in his *The Bella Coola Indians* (1948) picked Boas up on this. He questioned a number of Bella Coola in the early 1920s about Boas's picture of the upper heaven:

For some time no one could be found with knowledge of its existence. At length one of the older people remembered that a man who had died some thirty years ago had a personal story connected with it, and later a Kimsquit man was able to furnish definite information. He explained that in his family there was a myth dealing with this matter; others might have heard this myth, but since it was not their property, of course they would not be able to impart the facts contained in it, nor would they necessarily believe it. Consequently, an upper land, superimposed above that which is immediately over the earth, cannot be described as a Bella Coola belief; it is shared, so far as could be ascertained, by only two families (p. 25).

That's as close as McIlwraith comes to a damaging criticism of Boas in the whole of his two volumes. This murmur of dissent is crucial enough, however, to undermine the regal status of *The Mythology of the Bella Coola Indians,* "destined to become a classic in American anthropology," as one reviewer (with no knowledge of the Bella Coola himself) was ready to state.[4] The real classic, McIlwraith's two volumes, we will look at in due course. At least McIlwraith didn't try to get it all in ten days and from only one informant.

George Hunt

"I finished the texts with George Hunt," Boas wrote from Bella Coola on 5 August 1897, "two hundred and forty-four pages, and a number of songs on seventy-two more pages" (Rohner p. 219). Every morning he had been going over with Hunt in person the Kwakiutl language texts that had been mailed to New York. Every evening they had climbed a mountain together—"not as far as the top but just a few hundred feet" (Rohner p. 218). There is no doubt from the letters that he preferred the evening George Hunt to the morning George Hunt.

Hunt was born in February 1854 to a Scots father and a Tlingit mother. He was raised in Fort Rupert on Vancouver Island, with Kwakwala as his native tongue. During his first field trip of 1886, Boas stayed in Alert Bay with George Hunt's sister, Mrs. Spencer, married to the cannery operator; so if he didn't meet Hunt then, he certainly knew of him that early. On his second visit, Hunt was in Victoria, and they worked together on some unspecified matters. Boas was in Alert Bay again in 1889, and undoubtedly kept in touch with the Hunt family. He invited Hunt to lead a party of Native people to the World's Fair in Chicago in 1893. The winter of 1894 was the big potlatch at Fort Rupert and their intense collaboration

---

[4]W.J. McGee, review in *American Anthropologist* 1 (1899) 562-563. W.W. Newell's review in *Journal of American Folklore* 13 (1900) 153-155 finds parallels for the House of Myths in the Kwakiutl, using Boas's previous work. He has no independent stance from which to judge *The Mythology of the Bella Coola.* T.F. McIlwraith reviewing Boas's *Bella Bella Tales* (1932) in *American Anthropologist* 36 (1934) 606-607 is brief and kind.

over several weeks to produce the masterwork, *The Social Organization and Secret Societies of the Kwakiutl Indians* (1897). Hunt since then had been doing independent collection of texts; and Bella Coola was the place where his work was reviewed. They got together later during the 1897 Jesup trip at Rivers Inlet, and again in Alert Bay during July, August, and September 1900. Boas is now satisfied that Hunt's Kwakiutl material is ready for publication. Three months later in New York he dates the Introduction to *Kwakiutl Texts* 10 November 1900, and issues the first two hundred and seventy pages of text as *Memoirs of the American Museum of Natural History* Vol. 4 (January 1902), which later constitutes the first part of the Leiden 1905 Volume 3 of the Jesup Expedition, 532 pages total.

Let us take a look at this first publication of all their prolonged effort, the interlinear Kwakiutl texts by the master and his pupil. Since we must leave the language problems to one side, perhaps the question to ask about these stories in the first instance is: How do we like them?

The first story in *Kwakiutl Texts* (1905) is attached to the tribe of Kingcombe Inlet, specifically the Qawadiliqalas, whose first man of that name has a son famous for hunting mountain goats. He gets his power when he follows some mountain goats into their underground world through a trap door. When he arrives at the house where the mountain goats are dancing, Mouse comes out (four times) to tell him how to behave to gain power: he has to take hold of a feather being used in the ceremony. He enters the house, surprising them all (Mouse had told them he wasn't there). They put on their mountain goat skins by inserting the right arm first (an action now imitated by the Kwakiutl in putting on their costumes). There follows something about a wee dog in the youth's headband. The youth inserts the feather alongside the dog there, and leaves with surprisingly little trouble. On gaining the upper world he immediately kills four mountain-goats by waving the feather. (Then follows a page of instructions about cooking meat with hot stones, information that no Indian

George Hunt and his family at Fort Rupert, with visiting anthropologist. Photograph presumably taken by Mr. Hastings of Victoria in November 1894.

would dream of narrating to another Indian.) The story ends pathetically. After excelling in mountain goat hunting four times, the youth forgets one of the conditions of his power and cohabits with his fiancée. Then the "death-bringing" feather speaks: "It is bad. You made a mistake." Before the youth can get out of the house, he is changed into a grizzly bear. "Then he went inland. That is the end" (p. 25).

The original performance of this story undoubtedly had a great deal of pantomime, but there is no liveliness in this version on paper. I jump to *Kwakiutl Texts—Second Series* by Franz Boas and George Hunt, Vol. 10, pt. 1 of the Jesup Expedition (Vol. 14, pt. 1 of the *Memoirs of the American Museum of Natural History*) Leiden 1906 (reprint 1975), "Black-Bear-Woman and Grizzly-Bear-Woman" pp. 15-22. This story begins in an interesting way, characterizing the grizzly wife as lazy and the brown-bear wife as industrious (the latter gaining the favour of the husband, and making the grizzly wife jealous). The grizzly-mother comes home and tells the brown-bear children, "Your mother likes very much what she gathers," and then just proceeds to cook supper.[5] After the meal is served, the youngest child says, "Stop eating this meat, for it tastes like the breast of our mother!" From these hints one pieces together what has happened. If only this technique were deliberate! But, alas, it is a fluke, the fortuitous result of incompetence; for what follows is without artistry. The grizzly has served the meal and gone out for reasons unexplained. The black-bear children kill the grizzly children, again without motivation. They really should not have been wasting their time, especially as they prop the dead bodies in postures as though the grizzly children were performing routine acts around the house—obviously to put the grizzly mother on the wrong track and delay her discovery of the dead. But we are

---

[5]Again Hunt tells about the use of red-hot stones for cooking, an interpolation for the ethnologist rather than any imaginable Native audience. Perhaps a complete scrutiny of the Boas-Hunter correspondence will turn up occasions when Boas expostulated with Hunt on inconsistencies such as these.

not given that scene, and next see the grizzly in the middle of the chase. The bear is killed by a wren diving into her stomach and lighting a fire, so that she smokes at both ends. Her ashes become mosquitoes and horse flies (p. 22).

Hunt's myths and legends have never, to my knowledge, received evaluation. It appears that they are of not especially high quality, and that we will have to seek elsewhere for what is beautiful and wonderful in Northwest Indian mythology. If Hunt's texts were obviously inspired or engaging, we would delight that there are so many of them. Since they are apparently not, we can reshelve them with some relief, to await further assessment of the situation.

Boas's letters continually inject doubts as to Hunt's capabilities. His first mention of him, in Victoria, 13 June 1888, does not augur well for the future, since it involves a failure to keep an appointment (Rohner p. 91). Even during the Fort Rupert potlatch Boas could wish himself "away from here" because Hunt was so hard to get along with: "He acts exactly as he did in Chicago. He is too lazy to think, and that makes it disagreeable for me. I cannot change this, though, and have to make the best of it. He left at noon with some excuse and returned only after several hours. He knows exactly how I depend on him" (Rohner p. 183). At Bella Coola in 1897 the work with Hunt "is quite boring" (Rohner p. 216), and at Rivers Inlet, "The translation is going very slowly because Hunt is unbelievably clumsy with it" (Rohner p. 236). At Alert Bay in 1900 Boas feels fortunate to have another interpreter available to him, William Brotchie, referred to in the Introduction to *Kwakiutl Texts* (1902) as "a halfblood Nimkish . . . who made the translation of the Gospels for the Rev. Alfred J. Hall" (p. 3). Wherever there was a discrepancy between the opinions of Brotchie and Hunt, Boas took "pains to investigate the doubtful points" (p. 3). Towards the end of the season at Alert Bay, he is able to express a begrudging trust in Hunt: "I revised much of what he had done and can see that he does everything properly and that he does not pull my leg. I find him quite dependable, more than I had thought" (Rohner p.

261). I think Boas is talking here of the linguistics.[6] Texts which Hunt gave him dealing with hunting, fishing, canoe-making, and other aspects of everyday life, are obviously verifiable from common knowledge. Whether or not Hunt is reliable in the lore which is not capable of being checked is another matter. Boas did not hazard an opinion on the validity of Hunt's mythological texts, but simply presented them with an interminable dignity. Since Hunt was being paid by the page, there was likely some pulling of the leg somewhere. Hunt was given the role of informant as well as transcriber, and, hence, grounds for thinking that anything that came out of his head should be mailed to New York. Rohner interviewed Hunt's daughter in 1964, and, although her memory was vague in places, she gives convincing testimony to her father's methods:

> He used to go around each village to find out—find out the stories—the stories of the first generations to our people. And my father used to come home and write day and night. He used to be tired when he writes. He wasn't well educated, but he learned —learned all how it goes through nicely. And he made lot of the stories and sent it down to the museum at New York.[7]

---

[6]The Preface to *The Religion of the Kwakiutl* (1930) pp. ix-xii contains Boas's fullest account of his collaboration with Hunt; his reservations are concerned only with syntax and phonetics. Likewise the "Critical Remarks" Appendix to the two-volume *Ethnology of the Kwakiutl* (1921) pp. 1467-1473. See discussion by Leslie A. White in his *The Ethnography and Ethnology of Franz Boas* (Austin: Bulletin of the Texas Memorial Museum, No. 6, April 1963) pp. 30-34.

[7]Ronald P. Rohner "Franz Boas: Ethnographer on the Northwest Coast" in *Pioneers of American Anthropology* ed. June Helm (1966) p. 214. One gets a glimpse of a procedure Hunt sometimes used from his introduction to a family history in *Ethnology of the Kwakiutl* (1921): "I will only follow what was told me by my wife, who told me that story why the Awik!enox women have the name Abalone-Woman. Now, listen, friend! I shall imitate the way of all

Hunt was under Boas's orders to obtain material from all the divisions of the Kwakiutl. He got sixteen of the twenty; but something in the tone of his daughter's remarks makes one think he might have padded his dispatches or reassigned material on demand. At the very least, it seems apparent that he relied on his memory for a great deal of what he put down on paper. Until we have an expert assessment of his methods, it seems prudent to place the problem of George Hunt to one side.[8]

---

the story-tellers who tell the story to some one. This is the beginning" (p. 1261). Hunt then proceeds to tell his imitation, which is (not surprisingly) indistinguishable in style from the other stories he has supplied to Boas.

[8]In the bibliography of *The Ethnology of Franz Boas* (1969), Ronald P. Rohner listed under his own name a forthcoming study, "an Anthropologist's Anthropologist: George Hunt's Influence on the Ethnology of Franz Boas." According to a personal communication, Prof. Rohner does not now plan to finish that work. Irving Goldman used the manuscript collections for his *The Mouth of Heaven* (1975) and asserts: "The original texts in the hand of George Hunt and translated into basic English without the blurring effect of a grander generalizing vocabulary are very close to the original meanings, somewhat closer than the edited and published versions" (p. 11). He presents a few examples in the Introduction, but the matter is not taken up again. Wayne Suttles in a commentary in *American Anthropologist* 81 (1979) 96-98 challenges Goldman on his competence in the language, thus undermining his total contribution. "I suspect," he says, "that the Boas-Hunt five-foot shelf of Kwakiutl texts will never be used by anyone who has mastered them until Kwakiutl is taught as the Old World languages are and Kwakiutl texts are studied in the tradition of the Humanities, for their own intrinsic value rather than to serve some currently fashionable theoretical end" (p. 98). Robert D. Levine's comment in *Northwest Coast Texts* ed. Barry F. Carlson (1977) on Boas and Hunt is most guarded: "The results of their collaboration (in which the part of Hunt has not, I suspect, ever been fully recognized) was what seems to me the most brilliant analysis in the history of Amerindian studies in the years before the Second World war" (pp. 98-99). The implication that Hunt deserves more credit than hitherto granted him is a tantalizing remark. Stanley Walens' *Feasting with Cannibals* (Princeton University Press 1981) makes thorough use of the Boas-Hunt

In doing so, we are relieved of having to deal here with some 5,650 pages of manuscript material sent to Boas between 1896 and 1933, and all the published field work done when Boas was dependent on Hunt. The publications which are thus put in varying degrees of limbo are: (1) *Kwakiutl Texts* (1902-1905); (2) *Kwakiutl Texts—Second Series* (1906); (3) *Kwakiutl Tales* (1910), pp. 244-441; (4) *Tsimshian Mythology* (1916) pp. 888-935; (5) *Ethnology of the Kwakiutl* (1921); (6) *Contributions to the Ethnology of the Kwakiutl* (1925); and substantial amounts of (7) *The Religion of the Kwakiutl* (1930); (8) *Bella Bella Tales* (1932); and (9) *Kwakiutl Tales, New Series* (1935, 1943). In other words, Boas is drawing on Hunt's help to some extent for all his Kwakiutl volumes except *Bella Bella Texts* (1928)—and although Hunt is not mentioned in the Preface, he was present in 1897 and 1923 when the texts were collected by Boas, and thus probably had a hand in that volume too.

Henry W. Tate

Henry W. Tate, "a full-blood Indian of Port Simpson," sent Tsimshian mythological texts to Boas from about 1902 until his death in 1914. They were in the alphabet of Bishop Ridley's Tsimshian Gospels, and Tate supplied interlinear translation. For the publication of six long stories, with Tsimshian text, Boas employed Archie Dundas of New Metlakatla, Alaska, to provide him with the phonetics. "I should have preferred a revision of the texts with Mr. Tate," he says in the Introduction to *Tsimshian Texts (New Series)* (1912), "but this was not feasible" (p. 69). For the over three hundred pages of myths in *Tsimshiam Mythology* (1916) Boas simply revised Tate's interlinear renderings himself.

In the Preface to the *Tsimshian Mythology* volume, Boas warns us on two points in regard to its authenticity. First,

---

Kwakiutl material, but does not, however, risk scrutiny of "Hunt's diligence and scientific meticulousness" (p. 9).

Tate's tendency to bowdlerize: "Mr. Tate felt it incumbent upon himself to omit some of those traits of the myths of his people that seem inappropriate to us, and there is no doubt that in this respect the tales do not quite express the old type of Tsimshian traditions" (p. 31). Second, Tate's tendency to imitate published tales: "A few of the tales also bear evidence of the fact that Mr. Tate had read part of the collection of tales from the Kwakiutl published by myself in conjunction with Mr. George Hunt. A few others indicate his familiarity with my collection of tales from Nass River" (p. 31). In spite of these suppressions and imitations, however, Boas is ready to assert that "by far the greater part of the tales bear internal evidence of being a faithful record of the form in which the traditions are transmitted among the people" (p. 31). If we take the phrase "the greater part" to mean, as it literally does, somewhat over fifty percent, we are hardly reassured. *Tsimshian Mythology* is a magnificent volume, especially in its comparative mythology sections; but it is almost incredible that a scholar would base all that encyclopedic work on the missives of someone he had never met.[9]

---

[9]Since the preserved correspondence between Tate and Boas starts in 1907, well after the beginning of their association, it remains unclear how the collaboration was initiated. I have not inspected the interlinear translations provided by Tate, but his letters are ungrammatical, e.g. 7 June 1912:

> Dear Sir
> I received the money paid my storys on the last of May. Again I sent down some more four story I have sent it now which I hope you received them in safely and there four contains 103¼. Many white men come to me that I might sold them some but I told them that your take them as soon as I finish it. Very few storys more to me. But some war stories are many more yet if you want them. . . .

The exchange of letters is mainly about payments, and ends with 29 January 1914: "Received of Franz Boas the sum of $35.67 in payment for 117 pages of Tsimshian tales," just prior to Tate's death. See also

If the Hunt-Boas Kwakiutl mythology has escaped criticism, the Tate-Boas Tsimshian mythology has not. Marius Barbeau gave *Tsimshian Mythology* a thorough review in *American Anthropologist* 19 (1917) 548-563, and brought up damaging points. He disputed Boas's assertion that the volume "contains the bulk of the important traditions of the Tsimshian" (p. 31). *Tsimshian Mythology* represents well the general myths, such as the Raven cycle, which the Tsimshian shared with their neighbours, and which can be told by anybody; but it falls far short in being representative of the narratives that belong restrictively to a clan, a house, or a chief. Barbeau was basing his opinion on the field work he had just done with William Beynon at Port Simpson, where he did "an intensive field analysis of the Tsimshian social organization, supplemented by a large number of myths and relations—very few of which appear in *Tsimshian Mythology*" (p. 553). Barbeau thinks that Tate probably did not consult many outside his own family: "Hardly any of our twenty-five representative informants had been utilized by him. The fact that he himself belonged to the lower class (a Raven clan in the Gitzaxlel tribe, if we remember well) may not have made him *persona grata* with most of the chiefs" (p. 553). Tate's "corrosive diffidence," which limited the range of his stories, also affected his methodology:

> While in Port Simpson, we have learned that Tate was not in the habit of taking down the stories under dictation. He was loth to divulge to other natives that he was really writing them down at all. Our assistant Beynon knew only of his "keeping a little book at home for those things." The fact that he had made such a large collection was practically unknown in Port Simpson (p. 561).[10]

---

a Boas letter to Tate (28 March 1907) printed in *The Shaping of American Anthropology 1883-1911* ed. George W. Stocking (1974) p. 124, along with a letter to George Hunt pp. 125-127.

[10]Some of Beynon's letters are quoted by Marjorie Myers Halpin in "William Beynon, Ethnologist," ed. Margot Liberty *American Indian Intellectuals* (1978), where she gives a judicious comparison

Tate is here discovered to be doing what we conjectured Hunt did; that is, he engaged people in conversation or joined groups where stories were being told, stored the narratives in his memory, and wrote them down when he got home. Barbeau notes an instance of Tate's personal views being presented as though part of a traditional text, and therefore "misleading" (p. 562). Just how much of Tate's work is misleading we shall never know. Boas never knew; he chose to think that "by far the greater part" was all right. He committed an enormous number of man-hours to analyzing and categorizing and comparing the myths. He erected a monumental structure in *Tsimshian Mythology*. He did not, as far as I know, spend a moment to answer Barbeau's review, which plainly points out disturbing cracks and flaws.

Louis Shotridge

Shotridge, a full-blood Chilkat Indian, born at Kluckwan on the Chilkat River, was hired by G.B. Gordon, Director of the University of Pennsylvania Museum, in 1912, and was loaned to Boas in New York for the winter of 1914-15. Together they produced *Grammatical Notes on the Language of the Tlingit Indians* (Philadelphia: University Museum 1917), which includes a text written by Shotridge, "Origin of Mosquitoes" pp. 168-179.

Shotridge was then sent back to home territory for four years as a collector. The most interesting result of this field work for our purposes is "A Visit to the Tsimshian Indians" published in two parts of Vol. 10 of *The Museum Journal,* June 1919 and September 1919, especially the Tsimshian clan legend of pp. 122-131 presented with contextual background material. Shotridge was evidently not greatly influenced by Boas, and exhibits an exuberant individuality.

---

of Beynon and Tate as Native ethnologists (pp. 144-145). See also her 1973 University of British Columbia dissertation, *The Tsimshian Crest System,* especially pp. 119-120.

Chapter VI
Boas's Students in the Canadian West: Chamberlain, Swanton, and Sapir

Alexander Francis Chamberlain

Born in England and brought to Canada while still a child, A.F. Chamberlain was educated at the University of Toronto, and received his B.A. in Modern Languages in 1886. He was taken on the staff of University College, but partly through the influence of Sir Daniel Wilson chose to accept an appointment as fellow in Anthropology in the newly opened department under Boas at Clark University, Worcester, Massachusetts. This was in 1890; the following summer Boas arranged for him to go into the virgin territory of the Kootenays for the British Association for the Advancement of Science. His ethnographic report was published in the Reports for 1892. When Boas moved on from Clark that year, Chamberlain, now a Ph.D., was appointed his successor, and headed the department there until his premature death at the age of forty-nine in 1914.

Chamberlain published many articles concerned with linguistics, and was a work-horse as editor of the *Journal of American Folklore* from 1900 to 1908, and other journals in the discipline; but the trip to the Kootenays as a student in 1891 was his only field work, and provided the rather slender sheaf of tales that he has to his name. These were published posthumously by Boas, along with texts collected by himself in 1914, as *Kutenai Tales* (1918).[1] "The texts recorded by Chamberlain are brief," he comments in the Preface (p. v). "It should be remembered that these were recorded on the first field expedition ever undertaken by Dr. Chamberlain, and that it requires a considerable amount of practice to record long tales." Boas's tales in the volume are longer and better; it is almost as though he set out for the Kootenays four months after Chamberlain's death to get done what his old student had failed to do.

John Reed Swanton

Swanton's training and doctorate were from Harvard. As part of the standard Peabody apprenticeship, he was sent to one of the interminable diggings in Ohio, with half a following winter to wash skeletons in the museum basement. Putnam believed in young men learning their profession practically and manually. I assume he also had

---

[1] Franz Boas *Kutenai Tales* (Bureau of American Ethnology Bulletin 59, 1918) pp. 1-53. Some of these fragmentary tales had seen print previously. Chamberlain's linguistic care is evident in "Some Kutenai Linguistic Material" *American Anthropologist* 11 (1909) 13-26. See the full bibliography appended to the obituary by Albert N. Gilbertson in *American Anthropologist* 16 (1914) 337-348. Boas wrote the obituary in the *Journal of American Folklore* 27 (1914) 326-327. The work of Boas and Chamberlain with the Kootenay is briefly commented on in the preface to Harry Holbert Turney-High *Ethnography of the Kutenai* (Memoirs of the American Anthropological Association 56, 1941) p. 7, and also p. 189. This study from field work done in 1939-40 includes no stories, and only songs without words: "The Kutenai have no poetry" (p. 110). Turney-High published "Two Kutenai Stories" in *Journal of American Folklore* 54 (1941) 191-196, which are really anecdotes from Abraham Bull Robe of Dayton, Montana, whose bear myth was also recorded by Claude Schaeffer as "The Bear Foster Parent Tale: A Kutenai Version" *Journal of American Folklore* 60 (1947) 286-288.

Swanton at Pueblo Bonito under George Pepper for one of the many seasons there. The net effect seems to have been to drive Swanton away from archaeology.[2]

It drove him, as Kroeber goes on to say in this festschrift article, down to Columbia University and Franz Boas, with whom he studied linguistics while completing the requirements for his Ph.D. at Harvard, which he received in 1900. Immediately, in September 1900, Boas arranged for him to go to the Queen Charlotte Islands under the auspices of the Jesup Expedition. He spent ten months there, and returned to take up a post in the Bureau of American Ethnology, which became a lifetime appointment. In January 1904 the Bureau sent him to Alaska, Sitka and Wrangell, for four months. These two trips constitute Swanton's field work in the Northwest.[3] (His Southeastern U.S. and other work is, of course, outside of our purview.)

Swanton was a good student, an A+ student. No apologies are required for any aspect of his work. The stories collected on his first field trip are very substantial and presented immaculately. *Haida Texts and Myths, Skidegate Dialect*

---

[2]A.L. Kroeber "The Work of John R. Swanton," in *Essays in Historical Anthropology of North America* ("Published in Honor of John R. Swanton in Celebration of His Fortieth Year with the Smithsonian Institution") Smithsonian Miscellaneous Collections Vol. 100 (Washington, D.C. 25 May 1940) pp. 1-9, quotation pp. 1-2. It is an indication of how far Swanton's later interests took him from the Northwest that that area is not represented in the contributions to this festschrift.

[3]The full-scale ethnographic descriptions are contained in (1) *Contributions to the Ethnology of the Haida* (Jesup Publications 1905), and (2) "Social Conditions, Beliefs, and Linguistic Relationship of the Tlingit Indians," included in *26th Annual Report of the Bureau of American Ethnology* (1908) pp. 391-485. The 106 Tlingit narratives Swanton collected can be found in his *Tlingit Myths and Texts* (Bureau of American Ethnology Bulletin 39, 1909).

John R. Swanton. Frontispiece portrait from his festschrift, *Essays in Historical Anthropology of North America* (1940).

(Bureau of American Ethnology Bulletin 29, 1905) is an engaging and usable volume, as are the three other publications from this field work, *Contributions to the Ethnology of the Haida* (Jesup Expedition 1905), *Haida Texts — Masset Dialect* (Jesup Expedition 1908), and *Haida Songs* (American Ethnological Society 1912). I call them "engaging" and "usable" because, perhaps more than any other texts from this classic period of field collecting, Swanton's Haida material has attracted students and has been used by them. If we look at three instances of such use it will indicate how much Swanton has been valued.

The well-known contemporary poet, Gary Snyder, as an undergraduate at Reed College in 1951, turned to Swanton to try to do something that no one had attempted before: to look at a single myth from the viewpoint of all the accepted modes of studying folklore, to bear in on its meaning in relation to tribal culture, to world-wide legend motifs, to archetypal psychology, to the social function of myth, and so on. The legend he chose was from the *Haida Texts and Myths* (1905), "He who hunted birds in his father's village" (pp. 264-268), a version of the Swan-Maiden myth known throughout the world. Neither in the original thesis nor in the Foreword written for its recent publication[4] does Snyder say why he chose Swanton's rendition. The young Snyder's intellect was keen and wide-ranging, and the available texts were myriad: the mere fact that he chose as he did is a testimonial. That it supplied him with a book-length study without exhausting its ramifications is additional testimony.

Dell Hymes has used *Haida Songs* (1912) on two occasions for the close, sensitive reading that only he among contemporary scholars seems capable of. Hymes has the linguistic

---

[4]Gary Snyder *He Who Hunted Birds in His Father's Village: The Dimensions of a Haida Myth* (Bolinas, California: Grey Fox Press 1979). Another contemporary American poet, James Koller, has adapted songs from *Tlingit Myths and Texts* in a fairly successful ethnopoetic tribute to Swanton, in *Alcheringa* #2 (1971) pp. 31-34, reprinted in his *Poems for the Blue Sky* (1976).

resourcefulness to examine the original Haida text. He notes a few obscurities and inconsistencies, but in general confirms the adequacy of Swanton's interlinear translation. His challenge to Swanton is on the question of the real structure of the verse—he will, for instance, see seven lines where Swanton sees six—and the means of transmitting the effects of rhythm, repetition, and imagery in a free literary translation. "There is no law," he says, "that the first to examine a text exhausts it."

> Indeed, as can be argued in principle and supported from experience, a literary text is an open document, susceptible of different interpretation as the audience of interpreters differs, a document not necessarily exhausted by any one interpretation, but quite possibly enriched by many or all. Validity and interpretation have two aspects, the source and the receiver, and the exigencies of translation are such that any one translation is like a spotlight from one angle, highlighting some features, but shadowing others. A plurality of responsible translations can illumine more and in greater depth.[5]

I take this to be not so much a criticism of Swanton and his translations as a true statement of what is both annoying and inspiring about the whole process of translating: that it is

---

[5]Dell Hymes "Some North Pacific Coast Poems: a Problem in Anthropological Philology" *American Anthropologist* 67 (1965) 316-341, quotations from p. 335. In fairness to Boas we should mention that Hymes also uses four songs from *Ethnology of the Kwakiutl* (1921). Hymes's other brilliant work with Swanton's *Haida Songs* is his "Masset Mourning Songs" *Alcheringa* #2 (1971) 53-63. The former article is included in Hymes's *"In vain I tried to tell you"* (Philadelphia: University of Pittsburgh Press 1981), the latter not. A further close reading of Swanton is "Notes on Swanton Numbers 80 and 81" *Journal of American Folklore* 94 (1981) 358-364, where Richard Dauenhauer compares Swanton's handling of a Tlingit song with the translation of it in Margot Astrov's popular *American Indian Prose and Poetry* (New York: Capricorn Books 1962—originally published 1946 as *The Winged Serpent*).

never finished with—always providing that the original collecting of the text, with literal translation, and accompanying ethnographic information, is authentic. If Swanton's materials were not, in Hymes's opinion, authentic, he would soon have finished with them, and passed them over. As it is, he put them to such scrutiny and re-evaluation that his work with these Haida songs, the whole methodology so carefully and interestingly laid out, is probably the one place for a skeptical person to enter Northwest Indian literature; for Hymes supplies the kind of convincing commentary he will require. The publication of Indian texts is properly a triptych: (1) Native language, plus interlinear translation; (2) a careful free translation; and (3) notes on language and meaning. Hymes supplies all three superbly, because Swanton had already done so excellently.

The fourth factor which makes this a quaternary is the performance. We have already discussed the means by which Dennis Tedlock and others have tried to put on paper live performances. Is this factor completely null and void with the tales gathered and published long ago? Dell Hymes, working with Oregon and Washington myths, discerns a presentational form which seems best written down as poetic stanzas. Once the verse-like structure of the old prose narrative is determined, then there is the possibility of a new performance. As he said in his Presidential Address before the American Folklore Society in November 1974 in introducing one of Charles Cultee's Kathlamet tales: "The first performance to try to embody the presentational form of the original is tonight."[6] Swanton has not been used for this kind of structural analysis and presentation, but I am sure he could be.

Swanton has been used, by Wilson Duff, for an even more

---

[6]Dell Hymes "Folklore's Nature and the Sun's Myth" *Journal of American Folklore* 88 (1975) 345-369, quotation on p. 359. For the basis of the analysis of presentational form, see his similar treatment of another Washington Indian tale in his "Louis Simpson's 'The Deserted Boy'" *Poetics* 5 (1976) 119-155. The latter article is included in his *"In vain I tried to tell you"* (1981), the former not.

demanding test, however; for Duff tries to imaginatively reconstruct what a tale would mean to the teller and his audience—not just the obvious surface meaning but the deepest possible, one might say *philosophical* meaning. He uses a fictional framework: a present-day schoolboy in the Queen Charlottes is given an assignment by his teacher to investigate Swanton's story, "Raven Traveling"; naturally he consults his grandfather, who knew the original teller of the tale, John Sky.

> "That old man, John Sky. He was supposed to know a lot about the stars, the constellations, you know. He was kind of in charge of the old time calendar. There used to be a few of them did that: watched the stars, watched the weather, watched where the sun came up each day.
> "One time, I was just about your age, Ray, he spent a lot of time telling me this same story. It seemed pretty important to him. I guess it was because it's the story of how these Queen Charlotte Islands were created. Whether he believed it or not, I don't know. He tried to get me to learn it, you know. He explained a lot of things about it to me. . . . [7]

This technique of entering the mind of an old man who has special knowledge about the legends could be very inept or misleading in the hands of someone less expert and less sincere than Wilson Duff; but this unique ethnographic short story, "Nothing Comes Only In Pieces," is strangely moving because of its absolute conviction that something extremely important is being said by means of the images and symbols of John Sky's particular telling of the Raven Creation legend. Duff's trust in the wording that Swanton put down, phrases

---

[7]Wilson Duff "Nothing Comes Only in Pieces," included in the memorial volume for Duff, *The World Is As Sharp As A Knife*, edited by Donald Abbott (B.C. Provincial Museum 1981) pp. 315-324, quotation p. 318.

that most of us would dismiss as no longer capable of exegesis, i.e. such puzzles as "I am you. That is you"—this trust that the old written tale is valid and deserving of our best attention is touching. It should encourage other workers to emulate him in taking all the particulars of a myth seriously, and in assuming that the cosmology embedded in the mythology of the Pacific Coast is as intricate and subtle as our keenest intellect can imagine it to be. This kind of faith is only possible, of course, because there exist texts such as Swanton's, which have the intricacy and subtlety to justify the acts of imagination involved in such criticism.[8]

Edward Sapir

When R.W. Brock of the Geological Survey wrote to Boas from Ottawa on 9 May 1910 looking for a Head for the newly authorized Anthropology division within his government department, Boas replied: "Much to my regret, I cannot think of any Canadian whose experience and knowledge would justify recommendation."[9] Alexander Chamberlain is "of Canadian descent," but "I sent him once, a long time ago, to the Kootenay, which is his only field experience; and his

---

[8]Duff actually uses not the story itself as found in *Haida Myths and Texts* (1905) pp. 110ff but Swanton's retelling of it in *Contributions to the Ethnology of the Haida* (1905) pp. 72-74. The two tellings are very similar; but it is strange that Duff, so interested in the exact thought behind the words, should have chosen to use Swanton's paraphrase rather than those of John Sky himself. This circumstance does not, I believe, invalidate Duff's general intention with the passage, and what we can learn from it.

[9]This and the following quotations are from the nine-page letter from Boas to Brock dated 14 May 1910, from the microfilm of the Boas Professional Correspondence, American Philosophical Society, Philadelphia. Boas adds: "it seems to my mind that the few Canadians who are interested in anthropological research have not sufficient scientific training for the position that you intend to fill. I mention particularly Mr. Hill-Tout, who, besides, has a most remarkable ability of exasperating every one with whom he comes in contact, who is a good collector, but thoroughly unscientific in his conclusions."

interests are so strongly book interests, that he has been reluctant to avail himself of later opportunities to do field work." John Swanton is "amiable and an excellent worker," but "has not the qualities of a leader." The person whom Boas feels will fill the bill is Edward Sapir.

> Dr. Sapir is without any doubt the most brilliant among the younger anthropologists; and if you were to ask me for a recommendation, I should without hesitation pick him out as the man whom I should most confidently expect to develop the particular work you have in mind. He has had field experience among the tribes of Columbia River, of California, and of Utah, and he has been associated with me at Columbia University, with the University of California, the Bureau of Ethnology, and at present with the University of Pennsylvania, where he has also gained museum experience. The record of his work, wherever he has been, is excellent, and he has turned out a most incredible amount of material within a very short time. At the same time he has a most excellent critical mind, clear insight into ethnological problems, and ability to organize extended scientific investigation.

Brock was naturally impressed with this recommendation, and after a personal interview (with Boas, not with the candidate!) he offered Sapir, then twenty-six years old, the job.

Sapir proved to be a most brilliant man, of great and varied achievements, and of world-wide acclaim, though he died in mid-career in 1939.[10] His field work on the Northwest Coast

---

[10]Leslie Spier "Obituary" *Science* 89 (17 March 1939) 237-238; Ruth Benedict "Edward Sapir" *American Anthropologist* 41 (1939) 465-477. *Selected Writings of Edward Sapir* (University of California Press 1958) edited by David G. Mandelbaum includes a full bibliography. See also Richard J. Preston "Edward Sapir's Anthropology: Style, Structure, and Method" *American Anthropologist* 68 (Octo-

Edward Sapir. Frontispiece portrait from the memorial volume, *Language, Culture, and Personality* (1941).

constituted only a small amount of his total output. Even during his years as chief of the Anthropology division he was already working on his general introduction to the study of speech, published in 1921, as *Language* (still in print as a paperback today). Sapir's trips to British Columbia were brief: the first in the fall of 1910 just after his appointment, and the second, October 1913-January 1914, to the same place, Alberni, and the Nootka tribes living there. He trained a Native informant, Alex Thomas, who added further to the narrative material in the subsequent year or two until the total number of manuscript pages was about 1,250, according to the Summary Report of the Geological Survey (Ottawa 1915) p. 172. Except for one or two glimpses,[11] this material remained under wraps until Morris Swadesh, Sapir's assistant at Yale, pushed into print *Nootka Texts* (Linguistic Society of America, University of Pennsylvania, 1939) just before Sapir's death. In 1934-35, Alex Thomas visited Yale to assist in this.[12] The book is a beautiful memorial to Sapir's skillful field work and careful

---

ber 1966) 1105-1128, especially the discussion of Sapir's "life-history" or "personality-in-culture" approach (pp. 1120-1126), which, though stated much later, was operating during Sapir's Nootka studies.

[11]"A Flood Legend of the Nootka Indians of Vancouver Island" *Journal of American Folklore* 32 (1919) 351-355; "The Rival Whalers, a Nitinat Story (Nootka Text with Translation and Grammatical Analysis)" *International Journal of American Linguistics* 3 (1924) 76-102. See also "Songs for a Comox Dancing Mask" *Ethnos* 4 (April-June 1939) 49-55, an especially interesting item from Sapir's files, edited posthumously by Leslie Spier. There must be quite an amount of valuable material remaining in Sapir's field notes, despite Swadesh's editing of "Native Accounts of Nootka Ethnography" *Indiana University Research Center in Anthropology, Folklore, and Linguistics Publications* 1 (1955) 1-457. See also "Indian Legends from Vancouver Island" *Journal of American Folklore* 72 (1959) 106-114.

[12]See "biographical notes" in *t'a:t'a:qsapa (A Practical Orthography for Nootka)* by A. Thomas and E.Y. Arima (National Museum of Man 1970) p. vi. Thomas continued supplying texts and working on them up to his death in 1971.

scholarship. In the Introduction, Sapir thanks his informants, especially Tom Sayachapis, "an inexhaustible mine of native lore": "I cannot think back to his long hours of dictation without a resurgence of the affection and gratitude which he inspired in the old days of 'field work'" (p. 9). The stories are not especially great reading; in fact, the ethnological narratives are perhaps more vital; but the presentation and notes are completely reassuring as to their authenticity.

Sapir's field notes and scholarly example inspired a further magnificent piece of work, *Songs of the Nootka Indians of Western Vancouver Island* (Philadelphia: American Philosophical Society 1955). The sixty-seven songs recorded on a phonograph by Sapir in 1910 here receive the expert attention of musicologist Helen H. Roberts and linguist Morris Swadesh, both making use of further data from Alex Thomas. The "Notes on the Songs" (pp. 310-321) are especially interesting, as Sapir had obtained a prose rendering for each song, as well as the story behind the song, details of use, and matters of ownership.[13]

---

[13]See also Helen H. Roberts and Morris Swadesh "Songs of the Nootka Indians of Western Vancouver Island" *Midwest Folklore* 7 (1957) 134-136.

Chapter VII
The National Museum Men

One appreciates why Nansi Swayze entitled her book on Diamond Jenness, Marius Barbeau, and William Wintemberg *The Man Hunters* and wrote about them in a racy journalistic style. There is a natural urge to romanticize our pioneers. In Marius Barbeau's case there is some justification; he is a very suitable candidate for a large biographical volume.[1] One has only to think of his Quebec childhood, his Rhodes scholarship at Oxford, and, outside of anthropology, his work on Quebec

---

[1]Nansi Swayze on p. 139 of *The Man Hunters: Famous Canadian Anthropologists* (Toronto: Clarke, Irwin & Co. 1960) mentions Barbeau's just having completed his autobiography, which must be, like much more discussed below, still in manuscript. Hugh Kemp has preserved a lively picture of Barbeau at age 65 in his "Top Man in Totem Poles" *Maclean's Magazine* (1 May 1948). Clarisse Cardin's *Bio-bibliography de Marius Barbeau* (Ottawa 1947) is incomplete because of its early date, and awkwardly arranged. It is less useful to students of mythography than the selected bibliography appended to Israel J. Katz's obituary in *Ethnomusicology* 14 (1970) 129-142. See also Richard J. Preston "C. Marius Barbeau and the History of Canadian Anthropology" in the *Proceedings of the Canadian Ethnology Society* (No. 3, 1976) pp. 121-135, which quotes some of Wilson Duff's manuscript notes on conversations with Barbeau.

artists, and his interest in Emily Carr at a crucial time in her career,[2] to see how wide-ranging such a biography would be. In popular articles for the *Canadian Geographical Journal,* such as "How the Folk Songs of French Canada Were Discovered" (August 1954) and "Totems and Songs" (May 1955), Barbeau helped contribute to his image as scholar-adventurer. He was not shy on the public platform; and his enthusiasm in putting across not only his subject but also himself is evident in a Folkways Album (FG3502, 1957), *My Life in Recording Canadian-Indian Folklore,* where he talks, and sings, and beats a drum with the best of the "man-hunters." The real Barbeau will always be alive on that record.

However, there is a curse involved in trying to be popular in print; twenty years later you are still wearing a double-breasted suit and spats. In 1929 Barbeau got together with two big "names," Sir Ernest MacMillan and Duncan Campbell Scott, to provide sheet music of "Three Songs of the West Coast" for the Frederick Harris Company. This effort seems as pathetic now as any dated product of Tin Pan Alley. If Barbeau's "popular" books ever had readers, who today has heard of *The Indian Speaks* (1943), *Mountain Cloud* (1944), *Alaska Beckons* (1947), *Pathfinders in the North Pacific* (1958)? Even *The Downfall of Temlaham* (1928), republished as a "classic" by Hurtig in 1973, has not had success. It is a well-meaning book, but doomed by its flowery prose right from its opening sentence:

> Two messengers proceeded together from house to house in the morning, slowly as becomes the nephews of a proud chief on a ceremonial errand, their heads crowned with eagle's down, white like the snow and light as the air (p. 3).

How can one get past a sentence like the following?

---

[2]The story of Emily Carr's trip to Ottawa for a showing of her paintings at Barbeau's instigation is poignantly told in her *Hundreds and Thousands.*

Graceful and agile was her body and penetrating her black eye; her unspoilt mind was straight as a hemlock tree, a mind which had not once harboured hesitation (p. 7).

Not once? Someone gets a black eye for such prose. The second part of *The Downfall of Temlaham* is no better, even though the three long stories it contains are presented "realistically" as if told at a particular feast. In actual fact, they are compilations from a dozen or more informants (named in the notes), and are "freshly interpreted and paraphrased" (p. vii). The process is suspect, and is not vindicated by the result.

In two books Barbeau has hit it off very well. They have both been in print until recently, and should be reprinted. *Indian Days on the Western Prairies* (National Museum of Canada 1960) contains the narratives Barbeau picked up on his journey through Blackfoot country in 1926. It has a speed and vitality appropriate to the horseback warriors who are its subject. These legends, which are mainly exaggerations of real-life exploits, have an authentic ring to them. *Medicine Men on the North Pacific Coast* (National Museum of Canada 1958) is an idiosyncratic amalgam of pieces on shamanism; but it works. The "Swanassu Songs" of Isaac Tens are possibly the most interesting Native poetry *as poetry* in the whole corpus, all the better for our having the poet-shaman's own explication of them and their place in the story of his life.

Barbeau is most famous for his work on totem poles. But *Totem Poles of the Gitksan, Upper Skeena River, British Columbia* (National Museum of Canada 1929, reprint 1973) contains myths only in severe precis form.[3] The two-volume

---

[3] Mention should be made of Lieutenant George T. Emmons, who was stationed on the Alaska coast for many years and contributed ethnographic articles to the *American Anthropologist* and the *Journal of the American Museum of Natural History*. Pertinent here is his "Tsimshian Stories in Carved Wood" *American Museum Journal* 15 (1915) 363-366, since it gives three legends Emmons obtained from John Malo, "an old Kitksan at Hazelton, June 20, 1913," explaining a totem pole that is also discussed by Barbeau in *Totem*

Totem Poles (National Museum of Canada 1950) is better; but what substantial mythic narratives there are seem subordinate to the totem poles themselves. This may be quite proper for stories told about totem poles, but one ends up not

---

Poles of the Gitksan pp. 79-81. It is not only that Emmons's pleasantly told legends contrast with Barbeau's summaries, but also that there are surprising disparities between the two accounts of what the pole signifies. Emmons (p. 363) says it belongs to the Kish-hasht family, and represents

> first, the mountain goat painted white and black; second, the sun within which is the figure of the moose hunter, Kuke-shan, carrying a small basket; third, the monkey woman Pighish, and at the base the big horned owl (gwuk-gwu-nooks).

Barbeau, on the other hand, says (p. 80) that it belongs to the Gurhsan family, is called "Pole-of-the-Moon," and represents

> the Mountain-goat (*Mateeh*) with a single horn; the Moon (*Hlawqs*); (in the Moon) Skawah, the ancestress of the clan, with the earthquake (*Tsa-urh*) charm in her hand; (under the Moon) Legi-yuwen, one of the Skawah's sky-born sons, an ancestor of the clan; the Owl (*Gutkwee-nurhs*).

These accounts are as different as sun and moon! Barbeau had "long personal conversations" with Emmons in Prince Rupert in the summer of 1927 (p. 25). He was aware of Emmons's version, but we are left without any indication of what he thought of it. In these circumstances it is hard to define what a "reliable" text about a totem might be.

In this connection, mention might also be made of *The Wolf and the Raven: Totem Poles of Southeastern Alaska* (University of Washington Press 1948, reprinted 1961) by Viola E. Garfield and Linn A. Forrest, which includes some Haida poles. There have been a number of popular books on totems, notably Edward L. Keithahn *Monuments in Cedar* (1945, reprinted 1961), H.P. Corser *Totem Lore* (n.d.); Joseph H. Wherry *The Totem Pole Indians* (1964); and, locally, the Rev. G.H. Raley *A Monograph of the Totem Poles in Stanley Park* (Vancouver 1945), which acknowledges indebtedness for the stories of the poles to "Dr. Geo. Darby, Dr. Franz Boas, Mrs. Lizzie Wakus, Capt. Johnson Ike-ha-gwe, Mr. D.A. Bernard, Mr. Henry Moody Ske-dans" (p. 24). The definitive work on the relationship between totem poles and family legends has still to be written.

caring for that kind of story very much. Perhaps the typography and layout of these volumes has something to do with the feeling that the stories are compressed to serve as illustrative material only. *Totem Poles* was compiled after Barbeau had finished all his field work, and contains bits and pieces from five field trips. This makes it rather encyclopedic. One feels that his notes fresh from the field, without all the cutting and pasting, would be finer reading. Similarly, his *Haida Carvers in Argillite* (National Museum of Canada 1957; reprint 1974) is a fascinating "who's who," but makes no contribution to literature even broadly defined. Less than a third of *Haida Myths Illustrated in Argillite Carvings* (National Museum of Canada 1953) is Barbeau's, and of *Tsimsyan Myths* (National Museum of Canada 1961) nothing at all, a curious circumstance which will be explained in our discussion of William Beynon. The paucity of unequivocally authentic myth and legend in Barbeau's publications is strange but true.

The urge to popularization, even if it is only by one or two strokes of the pen, is treacherous to the thing itself. What the "thing itself" was we shall only know when Barbeau's papers are carefully reviewed. Wilson Duff did a preliminary examination with his "Contributions of Marius Barbeau to West Coast Ethnology" *Anthropologica* 6 (1964) 63-96, which put Barbeau's methodology under a cloud that no subsequent scholarship has cleared. Duff's crucial revelation is quite specific: whenever Barbeau told in print Chief Mountain's tale of the migration of the tribe, he left out the opening sentences, *as given in his own manuscript notes,* which reveal that the tribe began in the Nass country not in Siberia. Migration across the Bering Strait was a theory dear to Barbeau, so he apparently suppressed the beginning of the tribal history as actually told by Chief Mountain. Here it is, transcribed from the Barbeau papers by Duff:

> Our ancestors were at Leesems (Nass River) in
> the beginning. The flood came and they drifted
> away. . . . There were six canoes tied up together
> in the foam, it was not water. These were the canoes

> of *Gitxo'n* and his friends. *Gitxo'n* and his family
> drifted away. . . . Six canoes of our ancestors drifted
> outside Klawak. . . . They tried to find their way
> back to Leesems. . . . (p. 74)[4]

It is only *after* this point in his manuscript field notes that
Barbeau begins his printed versions. "Old Chief Mountain
would have been astounded," says Duff (p. 75). Whether or
not Duff intended to be so devastating is not clear; but when
he goes on in his article to undermine Barbeau's other favourite
theory—that totem poles are a recent phenomenon—one can
understand why his announced editing of the Barbeau papers
never came about. Did Barbeau really doctor a primary text
to fit a preconception? Further scholarship is required to
definitely settle the matter. And also the worrisome question
of how much damaging distortion resulted from Barbeau's
urge to make the stories attractive to his contemporary
audience. The texts seem more "readable" than they should;
Barbeau never supplied interlinear translations for legends,
as he did for songs; so that the whole textual question awaits
further examination.

The songs were obviously Barbeau's real passion, and we
should spend some time with them, even if it is mainly in
inexpert admiration. "Tsimshian Songs" constitutes Part 3 of
The Tsimshian: Their Arts and Music, edited by Marian W.
Smith for the American Ethnological Society (New York
1951).[5] Barbeau's presentation of these seventy-five songs is in

---

[4]The dots are Duff's; and it is rather unfortunate, in view of his
complaint about Barbeau's distortions, that he fails to indicate what
is omitted, and why.

[5]Parts 1 and 2 of this publication, essays by Viola Garfield and
Paul S. Wingert, were reprinted as *The Tsimshian Indians and
Their Arts* (University of Washington paperback, 1966); but Barbeau's
section was not included, and unhappily remains difficult to find. It
is a pity, too, that the film of Barbeau, with Dr. Ernest MacMillan,
collecting songs in the field (Nass River 1927) cannot at this time be
made available to the public because of shortage of funds for
processing. The titles that accompanied this silent film are transcribed,

Marius Barbeau, transcribing songs from the Edison phonograph.

three parts: first, an introduction in which he discusses the diversity of the songs and some of the singularities of the "Tsimsyan" (as he prefers to spell it). They were selected from 255 songs collected between the years 1915 and 1929, recorded on wax cylinders with a small Standard Edison phonograph. He gives short biographies of the twelve singers from the Nass and Upper Skeena who supplied the songs, glimpses that are much appreciated as one goes into the song-texts. The second section comprises commentary on the songs in the same order as the melodic transcriptions of the third section. These comments provide (a) free translations suggesting the literary and poetic quality of the songs; (b) literal translations; (c) musical analysis (done in 1938 by Marguerite Béclard d'Harcourt); and (d) miscellaneous notes "taken at the time the songs were recorded, including the name of the singer and the provenience of each song with details on its ritual use and personal implications" (p. 110). Even for someone without musical skills, this supporting information makes these songs among the most interesting texts emanating from the Northwest Coast.

As an example of how they engage one, and supply the means to stimulate one's own independent analysis, I would like to look at song #12; sung by Watserh (meaning Otter; English name Andrew Wilson) from Kisgagas, one of the two

---

along with a photograph, on pp. 72-75 of David W. Zimmerly *Museocinematography: Ethnographic Film Programs of the National Museum of Man, 1913-1973* (Ottawa 1974). "Tsimshian Songs" is, strangely, the only collection of Native songs Barbeau prepared for publication. When James Teit brought a delegation of chiefs to Ottawa in 1912 Barbeau took the opportunity to record their songs. In spite of these being "the best ever recorded in Canada," they still remain unpublished. Graham George gives a technical analysis of some of them in his "Songs of the Salish Indians of British Columbia" *International Folk Music Journal* 14 (1962) 22-29. Barbeau's three articles on the Tsimshian songs provide valuable background: (1) "Songs of the Northwest" *The Musical Quarterly* 19 (1933) 101-111; (2) "Indian Songs of the Northwest" *Canadian Music Journal* 2 (1957) 16-25; and (3) "Asiatic Survivals in Indian Songs" *The Musical Quarterly* 20 (1934) 107-116.

Lodzahut
(In the valley)

First note: C# (upper). Met. ♩ = 72 (Larghetto)

Record VII C 18 b (35)

Not transcribed to the end; very long song; upper notes extended to suit words.

TEXT

yɛ kweʼwilʼodȝáxut | ʼamaʼaxgodǝn | mǝxḷigǎʼi | yɛkce wilodȝaxute | hilʼen-
denkyeʼnéʼ⁵ | ʃkomatsmaxméqǝ | ʼaʃlaxgaxsganíst | sɛnǝ yɛhɛ | kcewilʼodȝa-
xute ‖ cḷegaⁱ | sɛnǝ ‖ cḷegaⁱ ʃkwilǝgǝm | wǒⁱ⁹ | nitamʼamagɛxtɪ | nitam yagahǝⁱ |
gu·n | sɛnǝ ‖ ʼyɛkcewilodȝaxut ‖ kweⁱtǝmdïtwilden | ʃaʼalgax | kumadȝɪlúʼlax | kʷü-
cemgŭcéʼliks | gǝlǝ²¹ | yɛkcewilodȝaxut

uppermost villages of the Gitksan, about 225 miles from the sea. "Blind, from an accident, he was only twenty-three years old in 1920 when his songs were recorded. His voice was remarkably high and clear" (p. 100).

Song No. 12: Lodzahut

a. As I look over the valley I am downhearted. I threw a stone at the small grouse in the mountains. . . (*Refrain:* — As I look over the valley. . .). I will weave anew the rotten fish basket, to use it again at the foothills. (*Refrain:* As I look. . .). I will not yield to the bidding of the small moth spirit to me.

b. Right here in the valley / will without heart / towards looking / right here in the valley // To throw stones I / small grouse / on the mountains / . . . / right here in the valley // To weave / . . . / to weave rotten / basket / will fix again to weave / will down from the hill use / now / . . . / right here in the valley // Wont will do / its speaking (its bidding) / small moth spirit / inviting or invitation / to me / right here in the valley.

c. Pentatonic; only one phrase, slightly altered upon repetition; great rhythmic flexibility. The rest on the beat is typical in many Indian styles—the quaver is followed by an accented semi-quaver. This melody seems to be in D (minor). Range: octave.

d. The singer, Watserh, a Gitksan of the Kisgagas tribe, gave the following explanation of this song.

A man sent his wife away. The blue grouse in the mountain represents her. He threw a stone and hit it. After hitting the grouse he sat down and looked over the valley, downhearted. He refashioned an old fish basket, to use it again in the valley. But when it was finished he cut it up in his distemper. He was making another when a bat flew towards him. Pushing it away he cried 'no, I don't want it!'

When the bat hits someone—according to a current belief—it is an invitation to come and die. The song begins after the bat has appeared. It is supposed to be from the grouse in the mountain—or the wife that has been dismissed by her former husband. It contains a threat: the bat will appear to him!

This Gitksan song is said to have originated at Kisgagas, but the singer was reluctant to give the particulars. Later, I learnt that it refers to an incident in the marital life of Dzeeus, of the Frog-Raven crest, at Kisgagas. The Grouse (*Pistae'i*) is a crest of his family. A long time after it was composed, the song was purchased "for a big price" by the people of the Wolf crest in the same tribe. It was interpreted by Mr. R.S. Sargent, a white man, of Hazelton.

The singer states quite plainly that the song is "from the grouse in the mountain" i.e. the wife who has been dismissed by her former husband. Mr. Sargent has been in Hazelton since 1891, but as an interpreter he was likely not entirely sensitive to a possible fluctuation of speaking voice in this song. It could be a dialogue between the husband and wife. I prefer to take it all the way over and give the song to the wife, who, though forlorn, is building up the power to threaten the man. I would give it a free translation as follows:

> Here in the valley
> With empty heart
> Looking back at you
> Here in the valley
>
> You threw stones at me
> The small grouse on the mountain
> From down in the valley
>
> I try to re-weave
> A rotted basket
> For us to use again
> Now in the valley

You will surely come
When the bat bids you
To me
Here in the valley.

Since the original Tsimshian words are available, and the
actual recording can be retrieved from the archives of the
National Museum, a future linguist might have something
further to say about this song, which, like many others in
"Tsimshian Songs," is provocatively beautiful and should
receive the best possible translation.

William Beynon, Ethnographer[6]

The care Barbeau took to make "Tsimshian Songs" clear,
attractive, and authentic indicates that he considered song
collecting the work for which he was best equipped and
would, in the end, be respected. Narrative collecting took
second place. In fact, all through the years from their first
collaboration in December 1914, it was Barbeau's "assistant,"
William Beynon, who supplied the best stories, working with
informants on his own account; and when we come to *Tsimsyan
Myths* (National Museums of Canada 1961) we discover that
the texts all came from William Beynon's independent work
during 1950-54, after Barbeau's retirement.

William Beynon (1888-1958) was born in Victoria of a
Welsh sea-captain and a Tsimshian woman of the Gitlan
group, whose father was Clah (Arthur Wellington).[7] Beynon

---

[6]In a brilliantly researched paper, Marjorie Myers Halpin success-
fully shows that Beynon deserves the epithet she gives him in her
title, "William Beynon, Ethnographer," in *American Indian Intellectuals* ed. Margot Liberty (West Publishing Company 1978) pp.
140-156, part of the Proceedings of the American Ethnological
Society for 1976. Beynon, she says, "did ethnography for White
anthropologists for over 40 years (1915-1956). Yet he is known to
anthropology, and identified in its literature, as 'informant and
interpreter'" (p. 141).

[7]It is interesting to read the information Beynon obtained from
his grandfather, which is printed (without, incidentally, any mention
of their relationship) in *Totem Poles* Vol. I pp. 41, 456 and 468.

learned Tsimshian from his mother, but found work in the white man's world (the Canadian Pacific Railway and the Department of Public Works) until he went to Port Simpson in 1913 for an uncle's funeral, and stayed there. Barbeau turned up in December 1914, and by 23 January 1915 could report back to Sapir in Ottawa that he had discovered "a very intelligent young half-breed," who

> records myths quite successfully and with good speed. He has them recited in Tsimshian and writes them down in English at once, sentence by sentence. The work could not be done any better if I were working with them.[8]

On returning to Ottawa, Barbeau made arrangements to pay Beynon fifty cents per page for field reports, and asked him to go to Kitkatla. In January 1916, after a shipwreck and other trials, Beynon settled in Kitkatla long enough to fill six notebooks. (They are still in Ottawa, intact.) Beynon was ill during 1916-17, but sent material to Barbeau in 1918, and was available to help in the second field trip of 1920. He was involved in all Barbeau's subsequent field trips, except possibly those of 1923, 1927, and 1939 (though there is no information that he was not).

Since Barbeau always credits Beynon's work, we can clearly see what he contributed to the various volumes:

The Downfall of Temlaham (1928). Eight of the twenty-eight versions of the legendary material used in this compilation were "recorded by" or "dictated to" Beynon. He was, in addition, chief interpreter for the stories Barbeau collected.

Totem Poles (1950). Among the many bits of recorded comment about totem poles in this two-volume work, one can reasonably identify thirty-two narratives of some substance. Eleven of them were recorded by Barbeau, with various interpreters, mainly Beynon. Twenty-one are credited to Beynon as independent recorder.

---

[8]Quoted in Halpin's article, p. 143.

William Beynon.

Haida Myths Illustrated in Argillite Carvings (1953). Barbeau has seven stories to Beynon's twenty-three. (In spite of the title, these myths were collected among the Tsimshian.)

Medicine Men on the North Pacific Coast (1958). Isaac Tens's important "Career of a Medicine Man" is attributed to Barbeau, with Beynon as interpreter. The other three stories in this volume were recorded by Beynon.

Tsimsyan Myths (1961). All fifteen texts were recorded by Beynon independently.

Beynon's narratives reached print through Barbeau's stenography and they are not really distinguishable in style, as we have them, from Barbeau's own. The need for scholarly scrutiny of the field materials is again called for. As entry into the presently published texts, however, one could not do better than follow Beynon's work with Edmund Patalas, an eighty-year-old man of the Kitimat tribe of Hartley Bay. In *Totem Poles* (Vol. I) Patalas supplied "Myth of Origin of the Eagles at Kitkata" (pp. 81-83), "The Grizzly-Bear Husband" (pp. 202-206), "Gunarhnesemgyet" (pp. 276-282), "Origin of Light" (pp. 334-336), and "The Caterpillar and the Girl" (pp. 367-369). In *Haida Myths* he supplied "The Giant Octopus and the Eagle Clan" (pp. 56-68) and "The Steelhead Salmon and the Child" (pp. 362-367). The latter is a long narrative, extracts of which had been used in *Totem Poles* (Vol. I pp. 176-177), where Barbeau's licence in re-writing is clearly evident.

According to Marjorie Halpin (her article p. 152), Beynon's supreme contribution to ethnology is a two-hundred-page account of an eight-day potlatch at Kitsegukla in 1945; obviously this should be published without delay. Also unpublished, she records, are "some 252 narrative and ethnographic reports" that Beynon sent to Franz Boas between 1932 and 1939 (p. 148). Beynon was to have gone to New York to visit Boas, but the trip did not materialize. Later Beynon worked for Philip Drucker, and in six handwritten volumes from 1953 to 1955 made "a synthesis of the *adaox* or traditional histories of the Houses of a number of Tsimshian groups" (p. 151), which also remain unpublished.

Diamond Jenness

Nansi Swayze tells the story of how Diamond Jenness was recruited into doing Anthropology for the Canadian Government. He had gone from the University of New Zealand to study classics at Oxford; he had met Barbeau there, and transferred a lot of his attention to Anthropology. He had done a year's field work independently on Goodenough Island, off New Guinea, where his brother-in-law was a missionary; and now he was back in his native Wellington, unemployed and recovering from a case of yellow fever. Unexpectedly he received a telegram "from a man named Edward Sapir in Ottawa, Canada." As near as he could recall to Nansi Swayze, the telegram read: "Will you join Stefansson Arctic Expedition and study Eskimo for three years? Reply collect." He had no idea, he says, who Sapir was, or Stefansson either, and went to the local library to find out. To make a long story short, he did go with Stefansson into the Arctic, for three years, 1913-16, and then joined the Ottawa staff, and ten years later took the place of the man who had sent him the telegram. Actually, he did not begin proper work for the Museum until 1920, having enlisted in the Canadian Field Artillery in 1917. The years 1920 to 1926, then, represent a most impressive effort on the part of someone who, to take him at his own evaluation, was a novice. The publications are very professional, and indicate that Jenness must have had from the start a great flair for field work.[9]

His real forte was biography. He was apparently a great listener, and usually managed to get down the deepest experiences of his informants, their religious life; so that what is most valuable to us in his work among the Carrier, for instance, is not the collection of "straight" tales, published as "Myths of the Carrier Indians of British Columbia," more

---

[9]Nansi Swayze *The Man Hunters* (1960) pp. 47-49. See also the obituary, with a full bibliography, by Henry B. Collins & William E. Taylor in *Arctic* 23 (1970) 71-81. *Pilot Not Commander* is the title of the special issue of *Anthropologica* edited by Pat and Jim Lotz as a festschrift for Jenness (Vol. 13 [1971] Nos. 1 & 2).

Diamond Jenness.

than a hundred and fifty pages of the *Journal of American Folklore* for April-September 1934 (pp. 99-257), and rather ordinary familiar stuff, but rather the long verbatim quotations throughout *The Carrier Indians of the Bulkley River: Their Social and Religious Life,* Anthropological Papers No. 25 from the Bureau of American Ethnology Bulletin 133 (1943) pp. 469-586, where it is apparent that the Carrier have wanted to talk freely to Jenness on such subjects as embarrassing confrontations with their Nass River neighbours, the significance of their personal crests, notions of the after-life, methods of acquiring guardian spirits, and shamanistic cures.[10] These accounts often go far beyond the normal results of soliciting ethnographic information. They create their own genre: anecdotal cosmology, the heartfelt and intricate display of a

---

[10]As with Barbeau's Isaac Tens, we see here the efficacy of songs themselves in the healing process. Or, looked at the other way, the healing process supplies the meaningful context for the songs, which are usually too short to offer literary possibilities. A tour de force of reportage is Jenness's account of a healing performance at Hagwilgate (pp. 572-576). The white school teacher had complained to the Indian agent in Hazelton about the drumming and singing, and Old Sam wanted Jenness present to substantiate their claim that the method of cure was neither improper nor harmful. The four songs used that evening were translated for him as follows:

(1) "A big beaver's nose goes inside the mountain."
(2) "Something goes into the water."
(3) "Many wolves come for something to eat."
(4) "The strong man afflicted by kyan is eating something."

Literary qualities, as we understand them, are lacking here. The use of the vague "something," for instance, runs quite counter to the concrete imagery we value in poems. Yet, to the participants that evening, the lines were obviously valuable in themselves, not just as hypnotic rhythms. It would have been useful if Jenness could have got from Old Sam the kind of explication Barbeau got from Isaac Tens. There are undoubtedly reasons for the efficacy of the imagery; Jenness did not learn them, but he unquestionably establishes the efficacy. (It should be noted that the same material constitutes "An Indian Method of Treating Hysteria," which Jenness published in *Primitive Man* 6 [1933] 13-20.)

coherent world view. Hence, the appropriateness of the word "faith" in the title of the most impressive gathering of such pieces, *The Faith of a Coast Salish Indian.* A born anecdotalist, Old Pierre of the Fraser River Katzie tribe, recorded this in 1936 with Jenness, and through the efforts of Wilson Duff and Wayne Suttles it was published as Anthropology in British Columbia Memoir No. 3 (1955). The myth-cycle called "The Katzie Book of Genesis" (Chapter II) has a breadth and variety of incident challenging in interest the Raven cycle of the Haida:

> In earlier times this Fraser River resembled an enormous dish that stored up food for all mankind; for the Indians flocked here from every quarter to catch the fish that abounded in its water. What I shall now relate to you about this land is not a mere fairy-tale, but the true history of my people, as it was taught me in my childhood by three old men whom my mother hired to instruct me (p. 10).

Old Pierre has style, and makes us feel that *The Corn Goddess and Other Tales from Indian Canada,* which Jenness put together for the National Parks Branch around the same time (1956), is a collection of mere fairy-tales compared with the important business here in hand. Old Pierre may not be a Homer, but he is certainly a Hesiod; and in *The Faith of a Coast Salish Indian* Diamond Jenness has enabled him to leave us his *Theogony* and his *Works and Days* in a readable permanent form.[11]

---

[11]Wayne Suttles's *Katzie Ethnographic Notes* published in tandem with *The Faith of a Coast Salish Indian* constitutes a remarkable corroboration of Old Pierre's cosmology by his son, Simon Pierre, who was the interpreter for Jenness during the 1936 visit and had vivid memories of everything pertinent to the event. Though Simon Pierre "has never attained anything of the fame his father had as a possessor of supernatural powers," Suttles in 1952 found him "a man of good humour, intelligence, and considerable knowledge" (p. 5). It is one of the happiest acts of scholarship imaginable which

T.F. McIlwraith

McIlwraith is the man R.W. Brock was really looking for in 1910, born in a reasonable sort of Canadian city (Hamilton, Ontario) and educated at an acceptable place (St. John's College, Cambridge), with a first class degree in Anthropology. But McIlwraith was just eleven years too late. When he needed a job in 1921, Sapir could only offer to finance field work. However, this turned out to be a blessing in disguise; for, deprived of anywhere else to hang his hat, McIlwraith spent more time with a single tribe than anyone had done on the Northwest Coast heretofore, and with his two-volume *The Bella Coola Indians* (University of Toronto Press 1948) produced an ethnography competing for completeness with those of permanent residents like Father Morice and James Teit.

McIlwraith was in Bella Coola for two periods, March to August 1922, and September 1923 to February 1924, an amount of time that proved to be just right. The first season he was lucky, lucky to find anyone at all in the village, never mind the two most intelligent and knowledgeable men of the tribe:

> Activities in the canneries would have interfered seriously with my work during the summer of 1922 if two men had not been confined to the village, Captain Schooner owing to an injured wrist, and Jim Pollard by the illness of his wife. These two men were willing to work half a day apiece without jealousy. Each was intensely proud of the traditions of his people and, realizing that their culture was passing away, was glad to assist in making it permanent in writing. An intimacy sprang up between Captain Schooner and myself culminating in my adoption, a circumstance which established and improved my position in the community (Vol. I p. x).

brings the father and the son together as theogonists in the same volume, which is (also happily) kept in print by the B.C. Provincial Museum.

In 1923 personal circumstances forced him to delay his departure, so that he got in on the winter dance season. Fate was again on his side. Even the death of Captain Schooner worked in his favour:

> it was suggested that I take his place, a proposition which I readily accepted. This admitted me to the ranks of the old men, and I imagine that my interest encouraged them to hold more ceremonials than they had done for several years (Vol. I pp. x-xi).

He mentions in a letter to Sapir that in his capacity as "prompter" he has made speeches in Bella Coola, and owns the (theoretical) right to kill anyone who errs in the ritual.[12] He also danced himself four or five times. This is an intimacy with the spiritual core of the tribe which a visitor might luckily fall into and which a resident might find difficult to live with on a permanent basis.

The placement of the mythology, etc. within the two volumes of *The Bella Coola Indians* is mainly by function. The chapter on "Religion" in Volume I, for instance, includes several myths illustrative of the prevailing attitude to supernatural beings and animals, notably a well-told Raven story by Jim

---

[12]I am indebted for this information to an unpublished paper, "A Study of Thomas Forsyth McIlwraith, a Canadian Anthropologist" by John Barker (University of British Columbia, April 1977). This is a thorough and perceptive survey of McIlwraith's life and work, and should be published. The obituary by S.D. Clark in the Minutes of the Proceedings of the Royal Society of Canada (1964), Section IV pp. 125-126, is affectionate and well-balanced, but rather short. Several elderly Bella Coola Indians today remember McIlwraith well, but only by one of the Indian names he was given, *Wina* ("Warrior"), derived from a legend about "Raven and the Berries" that McIlwraith enjoyed (personal communication from Randy Bouchard). Margaret Stott does not mention discussing McIlwraith with the Bella Coola people she met during her two months there in 1967, but her investigations, published in the Mercury Series as *Bella Coola Ceremony and Art* (Ottawa 1975), are an interesting confirmation of his work.

Pollard on the origin of death (Vol. I pp. 83-85). Although the texts of songs are given in Volume II under various headings, "initiation songs," "marriage songs," "mourning songs," "shaman songs," etc., the chief discussion of song-making occurs where it is most pertinent, in the chapter on "Rank," since new songs, freshly composed, are required each year for the elevation ceremonies:

> The father, or other relative, of one of those about to be received into the ranks of the *sisaok,* expounds in general terms the ancestral myth containing the name to be conferred, or will ask a fluent speaker to deputize for him. Another follows, until myths have been recited for all. The singers listen attentively, knowing that without further instruction they are expected to compose two songs for each person, embodying a few salient points in the myth, without exposing the details. . . . For several days the singers work at the songs. The principles governing their composition are identical for all types. At night, as he walks in the forest, or at any other time, a singer constantly tries to compose a tune. Others do the same, and at intervals they meet, either in some lonely spot or in the back-room of a house. Each singer who has composed a tune beats out its time, humming as he does so; then another gives his tune, and perhaps a third. After much discussion, which in some cases becomes acrimonious, it is decided what two tunes are best for so-and-so. Words are then supplied, a matter of less difficulty, all the singers assisting (Vol. I p. 199).

After his chapters on the rituals of the potlatch, McIlwraith presents some of the origin myths which are believed to authorize the rituals. He at first intended, he says in a footnote, to place all legends together in a separate section, but this "would have been contrary to Bella Coola thought since origin myths, for example, are regarded as entirely different

T.F. McIlwraith, with a group which includes Willie Mack, Joshua Moody, and Liza Mack. Harlan I. Smith took this photograph on his visit to Bella Coola in 1922. National Museum of Man, National Museums of Canada, negative #56872.

137

from either mere stories, or from incidents connected with shamans" (Vol. I p. 292). The chapter on "Origin Myths" (Vol. I Chapter VI) is where McIlwraith's work overlaps Boas's previous work somewhat. Indeed, because of Boas's *The Mythology of the Bella Coola Indians* (1898), he intended to pay little attention to the subject. The Bella Coola, however, were "so intensely proud of the deeds of their first forefathers that several insisted on recounting them before they were willing to do other work" (Vol. I p. 292). It is just as well, since McIlwraith obtained a more balanced view of things:

> Two myths may give different people as the first occupants of a certain village, nor does such con- tradiction trouble the Bella Coola. Each man, convinced of the authenticity of his own family account, is quite willing to believe that the one belonging to someone else is equally correct. . . . Boas (p. 61) likewise gives an instance of uncertainty as to the first occupants of a village, though, on the whole, he found Bella Coola mythology to be more codified than the present writer (Vol. I p. 294).

McIlwraith does not seem to suspect that Boas obtained his information from just one informant.

Or he chooses not to suspect. This is the only quarrel I have with McIlwraith: he does not let us know what he thinks about Boas's work.[13] There is the occasional footnote referring to Boas on some detail or other, but he neither uses Boas nor challenges him. "In the field," he says, "I deliberately dis- regarded published accounts" (Vol. I p. xii). There may be some justification for this in a descriptive, as opposed to comparative, ethnology, especially one that is running into two volumes. But he does not, to my knowledge, take up elsewhere the value of his distinguished predecessor's work.

---

[13]He calls Boas's study "the most comprehensive description of the tribe" (Vol. I p. xii), but that is not saying much if there is no other. One instance of "confrontation" with Boas has been dealt with in Chapter V above.

Perhaps he felt no need to do so when his basic mode of procedure was so clearly a silent criticism. Boas had not seen any of the Bella Coola rituals, and gives us an armchair account of the mythology. McIlwraith wherever possible treats the myth, legend, and song within the context of events and activities of the Bella Coola as he witnessed them and participated in them.

Recent National Museum Men

If Regna Darnell in "The Sapir Years at the National Museum" can end by saying: "the Division of Anthropology, headed by Diamond Jenness after Sapir's resignation, never again attained the prominence in anthropology which it had had previously,"[14] what can we say about the National Museum since Jenness? Tom McFeat searched through the reports of the Museum from 1909 to 1976, and found that "in the first decade of its existence the Museum was visible and its scientists salient; in the last both had disappeared altogether."[15] At present Ottawa is practically invisible on the Pacific coast—at least, as far as mythography is concerned. Of the excellent Mercury Series, only one title, Ridington's *Swan People* (1978), is directly pertinent to the concerns of this *Guide to B.C. Indian Myth and Legend* (see next chapter).

Addendum: The National Museum of Man Mercury Series has just published (1982) *Oowekeeno Oral Traditions* "as told by the Late Chief Simon Walkus Sr." The narrator tape-recorded these fifteen texts with Susanne Hilton in 1968; his daughter Evelyn Walkus Windsor, working with linguist John Rath in Bella Bella, turned to translating the texts in 1975; and the three people named brought the work to completion in 1980.

---

[14]*Proceedings of the Canadian Ethnology Society* (No. 3, 1976) p. 119.

[15]Tom McFeat "The National Museum and Canadian Anthropology" in *Proceedings of the Canadian Ethnology Society* (No. 3, 1976) pp. 147-174, quotation from p. 159.

Chapter VIII
B.C. Mythography Up to the Present

In this chapter we will look at the collectors of myth and
legend and song who do not fit into the categories of our
previous chapters, and whom we can loosely call "free-lancers."
Then we will try to bring the picture up to date, into a period
where expert linguistic scholarship has combined forces with
sympathetic and aware Native language speakers to perform
an amazing salvage job in myth as well as other data. We
include a survey of anthologies which have tried to represent
the myth and legend of this area.

I
Free-lancers

Edward Curtis, "Shadow-catcher"

Of the twenty volumes of Curtis's *The North American
Indian,* three include materials on B.C. Indians: Vol. 9
(1913)—Salish, particularly Cowichan (Curtis was at a potlatch
there in June 1910); Vol. 10 (1915)—Kwakiutl (the largest
volume of the twenty); and Vol. 11 (1916)—Nootka and Haida.
The mythology and other ethnographic information included

in these volumes is surprisingly good. Surprisingly, because
one thinks of Curtis as first and last a photographer. He was a
photographer first; but he was soon specializing in Indian
subjects, having as one of his earliest sitters the daughter of
Chief Seattle herself. He was the photographer on the Harriman
exploration team to Alaska, the beginning of a thirty-year
effort, aided by "men of letters and millionaires."[1] Theodore
Roosevelt became interested in his scheme for photographing
the "dying race," and introduced him to J. Pierpont Morgan.
One cannot help but think that his archival camera was
somehow supposed to exonerate the genocide.

Everyone feels the appeal of Curtis's photographs; it is a
combination of ethnographic fidelity and all-American gla-
mour. This is also true of the motion picture he made among
the Kwakiutl in 1914. A great deal of research went into it, a
great many authentic costumes and customs were utilized;
but the scenes were all staged à la Hollywood, and the plot
was no Indian myth but our own boy-meets-girl. It is, of
course, true that Northwest coast tribes took heads as trophies
of victory in engagements from time to time, but one is surely
thinking only of box-office if one entitles a film *In the Land of
the Head-Hunters*.[2]

That the mythology of the *North American Indian* volumes
largely escapes the posed quality of the visual materials is
probably due to the "valuable assistance and collaboration of

---

[1] The best way to get a sense of Curtis's achievement is to view the
film of his life, "The Shadow-Catcher," made by T.C. McLuhan.
But also see her introduction to *Portraits from North American
Indian Life* (A & W Visual Library 1972) pp. vii-xii. Quotation from
p. ix.

[2] The delicacy of Bill Holm and George I. Quimby is apparent in
their providing an altered title (*In the Land of the War Canoes*) for
the pieced-together remnants of the considerably damaged original
footage. See their *Edward Curtis in the Land of the War Canoes*
(1980), which takes us behind the scenes in the making of the film.
In the Land of the Head-Hunters was published by Curtis in 1915
(reprinted 1975). See also his *Indian Days of the Long Ago* (1915,
1975), which involves an interesting utilization of myth.

Photo courtesy of the Thomas Burke Memorial Washington State Museum, Seattle.

Edward Curtis at work on a camera angle.

Mr. W.E. Myers" (Vol. 11 p. xiii). Myers spent nearly twenty years with Curtis; he took shorthand and had "an uncanny ear for phonetics,"[3] undermining the old adage that a picture is worth more than a thousand words. I would be inclined to sacrifice a great many of the photographs before I would sacrifice any of the narratives.

Natalie Curtis

Natalie Curtis is not related to Edward Curtis, but she did, like Edward, get a letter of support from Theodore Roosevelt. It is printed in facsimile at the front of *The Indians' Book* (originally published 1907, second edition 1923, Dover paperback 1968). Except for that letter, the book is made up entirely of stories, songs, and drawings by Indians Natalie Curtis herself met and interviewed, mainly in the Plains and the Southwest. "By rail, by wagon, and by horse, over prairie and desert, the white friend journeyed from tribe to tribe, seeking the Indians with open friendship, and everywhere meeting their warm response" (p. xxi). Her one move into the Northwest (presumably by boat?) was to the Kwakiutl. She got a family totem story, and two songs, from Charles James Nowell (pp. 296-307).[4]

---

[3]T.C. McLuhan, cited above, p. x. Over ten thousand songs were recorded on wax rolls; seven hundred of them exist intact at the University of Indiana. Much information about Myers can be found in Florence Curtis Graybill and Victor Boesen *Edward Sheriff Curtis: Visions of a Vanishing Race* (New York 1976), especially in relation to the Kwakiutl sections, pp. 61-70. Curtis describes Myers, a former reporter on the Seattle *Star,* as sitting on his left hand, and an interpreter on his right: "I led in asking questions and Myers and the interpreter prompted me if I overlooked any important points . . . . Myers neatly typed his day's collection before going to bed" (pp. 29-30).

[4]See Frances R. Grant "World Loses Ardent Seeker of Truth in Natalie Curtis Burlin" *Musical America* 35 (1921) p. 47. Charles James Nowell is not to be confused with Philip Drucker's Kwakiutl informant, Charles E. Nowell, whose biography was published by C.S. Ford as *Smoke From Their Fires* (1941).

Frances Densmore

> I heard an Indian drum when I was very, very
> young. We lived in Red Wing, Minnesota, and our
> home commanded a view of the Mississippi River.
> Opposite the town, on an island, was a camp of
> Sioux Indians and at night, when they were dancing,
> we could hear the sound of the drum and see the
> flicker of their campfire. In the twilight I listened to
> these sounds, when I ought to have been going to
> sleep.[5]

It was at the age of twenty-six that Frances Densmore left
her conventional music training and turned again to those
drums. At the same World's Fair of 1893 which brought James
Deans and George Hunt to Chicago she heard the Kwakiutl
songs and spoke to musicologist James Fillmore. The scope of
her goal became almost as ambitious as Edward Curtis's: to
take her phonograph, as he took his camera, to every part of
North America. She too worked on inadequate funding, in
constant fear of its drying up (in her case, it was a year-to-year
contract with the Bureau of American Ethnology). She
published as many volumes as Curtis, and left a mass of tapes
and written materials in the Smithsonian Institution. Her last
field trip was in 1954, when, at the age of eighty-seven, she
visited reservations in the Everglades, and conducted a seminar
at the University of Florida. She died in 1957 where she was
born, at Red Wing, Minnesota. She had kept a diary daily
from the moment of her visit to Chicago in 1893 until the day
of her death.

Two field trips brought her into contact with B.C. Indians;
she was at Neah Bay on the Olympic Peninsula of Washington

---

[5]Frances Densmore, quoted by Charles Hofmann in the Introduction to his memorial compilation, *Frances Densmore and American Indian Music* (New York; Museum of the American Indian,
Heye Foundation 1968) p. 1. Bibliographical information may also
be found in Gertrude Kurath's "Memorial to Frances Densmore"
Journal of Ethnomusicology 2 (1958) 70-71.

Frances Densmore. Frontispiece portrait from the memorial volume, *Frances Densmore and American Indian Music* (1968).

in the summers of 1923 and 1926, and in September of the latter year took the opportunity to visit the hop-fields of Chilliwack, B.C., where about a thousand Indians from many different parts of the Province were at work on the harvest. On p. 12 of *Music of the Indians of British Columbia* (published as one of the Anthropological Papers No. 27, Bureau of American Ethnology Bulletin 136, 1943, pp. 1-99) Densmore lists the twenty-one singers represented in the volume, their home reserves, and the number of songs sung, totalling ninety-eight (out of 121 recorded). In her customary fashion, she gives the musical notation for each song, and a musical analysis in technical language; but she also introduces the singer to us with some personal details, and in layman's language goes into the circumstances surrounding the singing and its original function in the tribe. In this volume the most interesting items are the *slahal* gambling songs and the discussion of them, and the healing songs sung by Tasalt, otherwise known as Catholic Tommy, and perhaps most of all the "Dance Songs" of Dennis Peters. In the Spirit Dance revival of recent years, the songs of an individual's visionary experience have become a sacred, not-to-be-divulged possession of the dancer, under protection and penalty of tribal edict. Three of these spirit dance songs are actually included in the tape available from the Archive of Folk Song, Music Division of the Library of Congress.[6]

The "Songs Connected with Stories" section is rather meagre, but in the prior publication *Nootka and Quileute Music* (Bureau of American Ethnology Bulletin 124, 1939) the supporting information for the songs, including any stories or myths involved, is quite extensive, notably the section on whaling pp. 47-72. Since the songs of this volume were collected at Neah Bay, Washington, Makah singers predominate in the Nootka language section, but two women who had married into the Makah tribe from Clayoquot on the West coast of

---

[6]As sent to Oliver Wells, Sardis, in the late sixties. This aural evidence has been overlooked in the scholarly works on spirit dancing.

Vancouver Island, Mrs. Sarah Guy and Mrs. Alice Long Tom, give a substantial and varied sampling of their songs, and represent British Columbia very well.[7]

Ida Halpern

Ida Halpern was born in Vienna, and received her Doctorate in Musicology at the University there. She arrived in British Columbia in 1939 via a lectureship in Music at the University of Shanghai. She is cosmopolitan in background. When her curiosity about local Indian music leads her into this new area of specialization, she treats a Kwakiutl or Nootka potlatch song no less respectfully than if it had been composed in Europe. Through the alertness of Folkways Records of New York, she has been able to publish in three albums an aural anthology of the best Native singers of our time. She has not published a book, but the printed notes which accompany the records are the equivalent.[8] There we are introduced to all the singers and the individual songs. Ida Halpern has a warm, colourful manner in presenting the life-events and opinions of the people she met and recorded, especially Billy Assu of Cape Mudge (she was his guest there on several visits from 1947 up to his death in 1965) and Mungo Martin of Fort Rupert, who was recorded at weekly visits to Dr. Halpern's house during the period he was working on restoration of totem poles for the University of British Columbia in the 1950s. These men were very important people in their world; it is an achievement to have gained their friendship and been the agency by which their voice is passed on. One memorable quotation in particular sums up Dr. Halpern's contribution:

---

[7]*Songs of the Nootka and Quileute* is available as Library of Congress Recording AAFS L32 (1952), in the Folk Music of the United States series.

[8]*Indian Music of the Pacific Northwest Coast* (Folkways Records Album No. FE4523, 1967); *Nootka* (Ethnic Folkways Library Album No. FE4524, 1974); and *Kwakiutl* (Album No. FE4122, 1981). See the review by Linda J. Goodman in *Ethnomusicology* 25 (January 1981) 162-165.

when **reproached by other** chiefs for having given away his songs, **Mungo Martin said,** "I was a sick man when starting to sing for her. Now after a year's singing I sang myself to health and am well again."[9] For the interested member of the general public, there is no better way of diving into the strange experience of Indian music—certainly no more convenient way—than to sample the *Indian Music of the Pacific Northwest Coast* (Folkways 1967) with the accompanying booklet in hand. And if one feels that too much of an Indian song seems to be meaningless syllables, Ida Halpern comes to one's rescue in an interesting article in *Ethnomusicology* 20 (1976) pp. 253-271, "On the Interpretation of 'Meaningless-Nonsensical Syllables' in the Music of the Pacific Northwest Indians." What is notable about this article is Dr. Halpern's loyalty to the singers and their songs. She insists that they receive not one iota of unjustified disparagement. The phrases in question are seen as equivalent to our "hallelujah":

> In the example of Hallelujah, we know the derivation of the word from the Greek "alleouia" and the Hebrew "halaluyah," meaning "Praise ye Jehova" . . . but would another culture comprehend it if it were not written down? My point is (no sacrilege intended) could not another culture interpret, for instance, Handel's "Hallelujah" as "meaningless syllables"? (p. 270)

Norman Lerman

"The Chilliwack seem to possess but few folk-tales, or else they have forgotten them" (*The Salish People* Vol. 3, p. 58). Hill-Tout was here relying on Captain John of Soowahlie, who, as an aide to Rev. Crosby for many years, had undoubtedly suppressed from his memory the old pagan stories. They were still around. Norman Lerman found many of them in his

---

[9]*Indian Music of the Pacific Northwest Coast* (Folkways 1967) notes p. 4. Mungo Martin sang 124 songs, fourteen of which are included in the album.

two months' field work in the summer of 1950.

What Lerman did was very straightforward. He wanted to demonstrate his qualifications for entering graduate school in the Anthropology Department of the University of Washington, and Erna Gunther advised him to gather some original ethnographic data, and told him where it could be found. Harry Uslick and his wife, and Bob Joe and his wife, were quite willing to spend days on end with him in Chilliwack. He was also interested in getting different versions from different places, and gathered analogues in Everson, Washington, and in Tsawwassen and Musqueam. He took all the stories down in longhand English. "Every word said by the informants was put down as faithfully as possible. The changes made were the correction of grammar, and the occasional changing of the personal pronoun for the actual name of the person."[10] Lerman must have been easy to talk to: the stories are unusually full and flowing. Seven stories with variants (up to four variants in some cases) are presented with commentary in his subsequent M.A. thesis (1952), which is well worth obtaining from the University of Washington.

The publications resulting from his work are less satisfactory; in both cases he collaborated with a professional author to rewrite the stories for the so-called "larger audience." *Once Upon an Indian Tale* with Helen S. Carkin (1968) slants seven stories towards the junior level. It is a pleasant enough book, and most of the stories are not found in the thesis. *Legends of the River People* (1976) also includes much material not previously available. Here the work of the co-author, Betty Keller, is quite ambitious: she has set thirty of Lerman's stories in a framework, where one is asked to imagine their being told in a family reunion setting. There is interaction between the old storytellers and the children around the fire, and a thematic arrangement for each of the five days of the get-together. This is a brave try at adding authenticity by

---

[10]Norman Hart Lerman *An Analysis of Folktales of Lower Fraser Indians, British Columbia* (M.A. Thesis, University of Washington 1952) p. 4.

dramatic verisimilitude. It works, up to a point: one does not really become involved in the linkages, but there is a feeling that that's the way it would most certainly have been in the old days.

Norman Lerman was born in Winnipeg in 1926, and wrote the preface to *Legends of the River People* just prior to his early death in October 1975. He had other interests besides folklore, which meant he never managed the full-scale publication that his youthful field work deserves.

Wilson Duff and the Sxwaixwe Myth

It is strange that Lerman did not apparently obtain the distinctively Stalo story of the sxwaixwe mask. Hill-Tout did; and his version was picked up by Helen Codere in "The Swai'xwe Myth of the Middle Fraser River: the Integration of Two Northwest Coast Cultural Ideas" *Journal of American Folklore* 61 (1948) 1-18, to which she added the version obtained from Bob Joe by Marian W. Smith in 1938 and her own version recorded from Mrs. Bertha Peters in 1945. Jenness printed Old Pierre's rather brief treatment of the subject in *The Faith of a Coast Salish Indian* (1955) pp. 11-12, 71-72, and other Coast Salish versions in an appendix pp. 91-92. Wilson Duff's one notable contribution to Stalo mythography is his presentation of Mrs. Robert Joe's account of the sxwaixwe, the fullest extant, with his provocative questions about the mask and its origin, in *The Upper Stalo Indians* (1952) pp. 123-126.

Duff does not, however, settle any of the problems. Here is a mask, apparently the one true Coast Salish mask, associated in its origin with a young man who has a loathsome skin disease and who intends to commit suicide by drowning. He is cured by the creatures of the underwater in a reciprocal healing. Later, the mask and paraphernalia are acquired from the depths, being fished out by the young man's sister, and passed on through her. There are many psychological oddities about this story and about the mask itself, whose most distinctive feature is the bulging out of the eyes and tongue. The myth represents one of the great outstanding challenges to interpretation. Duff's conclusion that "the sxwaixwe resembles the ritual display privileges of the Nootka," and in conception and function "could easily have developed from one of these" (p. 126) does not do justice to the deeply troubled state of the protagonist in the myth and the healing ("washing")[11] uses to which the mask is put.

Oliver Wells of Edenbank Farm

Oliver Wells talked to Bob Joe at some length about the sxwaixwe myth in 1964; but, since he chose to reprint Mrs. Joe's version, via Duff, in his *Myths and Legends of the Staw-loh Indians* (1970), interesting additional material will await the publication of the transcribed tapes of his interviews.[12]

---

[11]Homer G. Barnett *The Coast Salish of British Columbia* (University of Oregon 1955; reprinted 1975) pp. 158-159; see also "Sickness and Death," pp. 209-222. Barnett does not present the sxwaixwe legend, apparently considering the mythological aspect relatively unimportant. Philip Drucker's *The Northern and Central Nootkan Tribes* (Bureau of American Ethnology Bulletin 144, 1951) referred to by Duff in connection with his Nootka comment, focusses on "the bases of social stratification" (p. 1) and, like Barnett, mainly ignores myth, presenting only a sampling to illustrate belief in the supernatural (pp. 157-163). The pages referred to by Duff, pp. 256-260, portray a people "inordinately fond of festivities" (p. 257); behind the Nootka "display privileges" resides, it would seem, a motive quite alien to the sxwaixwe experience.

In the recently published anthology in honour of Wilson Duff, George F. MacDonald of the National Museum of Man writes with great perspicuity on the *swaihwe* (his spelling) in "Cosmic Equations in Northwest Coast Indian Art" (*The World is as Sharp as a Knife* ed. Donald N. Abbott, B.C. Provincial Museum 1981, pp. 225-238). It is impossible here to do justice to his impressive insights in equating the mask with housefronts, Chilcat blankets, coppers, and shamans' mirrors.

[12]Oliver Wells's daughter, Mrs. Marie Weeden, is working with Ralph Maud and Brent Galloway to prepare for publication a verbatim transcript of all the taped interviews, estimated to exceed six hundred typescript pages.

Of the legends he himself obtained and published in the above collection, the stories of Dan Milo are outstanding. Milo was over ninety years old when Wells talked to him, and was obviously very pleased to sing and tell stories in the Halkomelem language and in English translation. It is unfair to judge Milo's performance by the small extracts published; but in this Stalo pamphlet and in his *Squamish Legends* (1966) — similar extracts from interviews with Chief August Jack Khahtsahlano and Domanic Charlie — one gets a strong sense of Wells's sincerity and the value of the further material to come.

Oliver Wells's death in 1970 brought to an end ten years of ethnographic work with the Native people of the Chilliwack area, where he was the third-generation proprietor of Edenbank Farm. In his ability to put a lifetime's experience of the valley into his questions, Wells was a unique interviewer. The Indians knew that he knew what he was talking about. He had walked the same trails, ridden them on horseback. The old informants had known his father and grandfather, had in some cases been employed on the farm, had seen Oliver grow up there. And Wells, once he turned to a systematic study of the tribes, had a persistent curiosity. With his brother, Casey Wells, he compiled and published *A Vocabulary of Native Words in the Halkomelem Language* (1965). He documented Salish weaving, and brought about its revival. He supervised the building of nine native canoes, photographing the work at all its stages. And he managed to get Dan Milo, Bob Joe, Mrs. August Jim, and others, on tape, speaking conversational Halkomelem in a natural setting and performing stories for him as they might before a proper audience, which he proved himself to be.

The Sepass Poems

When at last the Chief spoke to me, it was to tell me that he had decided to give me, Eloise Street, his songs which were his own and known only to himself; he exacted from me a solemn promise that I should have them published in a book, so that his people would not forget their great past. I promised, and after that during the next four years, he spent day after day in our home, reciting the old words slowly to my mother, translating them into Chilliwack, which my mother understood and spoke fluently, discussing meanings with her in the Chilliwack dialect, Chinook, or smatterings of English, going over and over it until the sense of the passage was clear, then when both were satisfied as to meaning, my mother offered a translation and I wrote it down.

Thus came into existence the *Sepass Tales*.[13] Chief Billy Sepass was an imposing figure in the Chilliwack Valley in his time, and had roots in a much larger Indian history, conceivably in a tradition of sun-worship, as Eloise Street claims; so that his sacred testament should be of utmost concern to us. The reason we hesitate to grant it our immediate credulity is that the volume is prefaced by speculative clap-trap from the pen of someone who signs himself "Chief Waupauka LaHurreau (Shup-She)" and whose photograph is not reassuring. Furthermore, while some of the songs are recognizable renditions of Coast Salish Transformer themes, and the theft of the salmon baby is specifically a favourite Fraser River story, there is a more mystical aspect to this material, which does not to my knowledge have a counterpart, even in "The Katzie Book of Genesis" (see Diamond Jenness *The Faith of a Coast Salish Indian,* Chapter II). According to Sepass the world was created through a love-match of the sun and moon, when "their souls burned with a white flame of longing" (*Sepass Tales* p. 31). Of

---

[13]Eloise Street entitled them *Sepass Poems* in a preliminary mimeographed publication in 1957, where the process of translation is described in more detail than in the Foreword to *Sepass Tales* (1963, reprinted 1974 by the Sepass Trust, Chilliwack, B.C.). The quotation is from p. 7 of the "Glossary" section of the 1957 publication, where she indicates (p. 4) that the original translation "was done lefthanded in paragraph blocks, marked for line endings.... With no knowledge of the value of first records, these were replaced by the typed copies and destroyed as useless."

course, this is Sepass through the mediumship of Mrs. Street, daughter of Rev. Edward White, and graduate of Hamilton Ladies' College, Ontario.

Yet, at the same time, the poems would be even more suspect if they were not in what Eloise Street acknowledges is the "slightly Victorian English" of a person of her mother's education and time. And she goes on, in the 1957 mimeograph edition (pp. 7-8), to give personal witness to the pains that were taken over the translation:

> I read it aloud then and the Chief listened closely to make sure the syllable stresses and length of line were as they should be. He accepted my mother's translation from the Indian he understood into English words, most of which were meaningless to him. This shows the position of confidence my mother had reached with the Indians around her. He judged the lines by sound, and when he was satisfied, the line was passed as completed.

In view of Dell Hymes's recent proposition (discussed elsewhere in this volume) that North American Indian narrative, at its best, is clearly verse drama, this unique picture of an informant insisting that the translation be in verse, and exactly to his specifications, has great value as confirmation. Eloise Street seems to understand the importance of this, and repeats the point:

> He now had to be satisfied that the translation was correct in meaning and that each line had the same syllable length as his original, and had the same stresses. It took a highly flexible English vocabulary to do this, and a great deal of time, but in the end both were satisfied (1957 edition, p. 1).

The result is hardly satisfying to the modern reader as verse, but on the basis of Eloise Street's testimony we might be in danger of missing the uniquely authentic essence if we allow ourselves to be put off by the atrociously romantic externals.

Apparently the first stage of the translation process was that Chief Sepass had to recite the narratives "as he had learned them in what he claimed was an ancient Indian tongue" (1957 edition p. 1):

> It was a sort of free verse, rather like waves washing on a beach, rolling in and withdrawing, rolling in again and again. These lines were spoken in a semichant, the singer holding in one hand a small drum, which he palmed with the other hand. A traditional form governed the delivery. As the mood dictated, he would stand still and declaim in an oratorial style, then his chant would turn into a lively falsetto singing, accompanied by dance steps. Sequence followed sequence in this manner, the phrases having always an uplift of voice at the end, which had the effect of drawing the listener on with a sense of continuance—of something never quite finished—again like the sound of waves (1957 edition p. 8).

The *Sepass Tales,* which unfortunately do not draw the listener on, represent possibly the most lamentable loss in transmission of all the materials surveyed in this *Guide.*

Pauline Johnson

Or perhaps *Legends of Vancouver* is an even greater loss, all the more lamentable because of its popularity. The legends were originally printed in the Vancouver *Province* in 1911; they have been published in book form twelve times in four separate editions, and since 1961 in paperback from McClelland and Stewart. Everyone can agree that Pauline Johnson is a marvellously emotive writer, and that Chief Joe Capilano's Flood story, for instance, should be as moving as Hill-Tout recorded that Mulks's was; but it is a question of degree. In Pauline Johnson's supposedly verbatim rendition of Chief Joe, the milk of human kindness flows like the flood waters themselves:

Then with the bravest hearts that ever beat, noble hands lifted every child of the tribe into this vast canoe; not one single baby was overlooked. The canoe was stocked with food and fresh water, and lastly, the ancient men and women of the race selected as guardians to these children the bravest, most stalwart, handsomest young man of the tribe, and the mother of the youngest baby in the camp— she was but a girl of sixteen, her child but two weeks old; but she, too, was brave and very beautiful. These two were placed, she at the bow of the canoe to watch, he at the stern to guide, and all the little children crowded between.

And still the sea crept up, and up, and up. At the crest of the bluffs about Lake Beautiful the doomed tribes crowded. Not a single person attempted to enter the canoe. There was no wailing, no crying out for safety. "Let the little children, the young mother, and the bravest and best of our young men live," was all the farewell those in the canoe heard. . .
(1961 edition, pp. 72-73).

Chief Joe died before this version got into print. One wonders if he would have recognized it as his.

Pauline Johnson was a great entertainment personality in her time. She gained her fame as the "sweet Mohawk singer," and crossed the continent several times in fifteen years of platform appearances—but, in the words of her latest editor in the Introduction to *Legends of Vancouver* (1961), "abusing her great poetic gifts by turning out topical and jingoistic doggerel that served its purpose well but is worthless now" (p. xiii). Settling in Vancouver in 1909, she cultivated Chief Joe Capilano's friendship during the last year of his life, when she too was already sick and approaching death. One has to decide whether or not her use of Squamish materials is in keeping with her life as an entertainer, accommodating Indian lore to white man's commonplace sentimentalities. She is masterful in what she does, almost convincing us that Chief

Joe came to visit her in a deluge of rain, and that the following conversation ensued:

> . . . he remarked it was not so very bad, as one could yet walk.
>
> "Fortunately, yes, for I cannot swim," I told him.
>
> He laughed, replying, "Well, it is not so bad as when the Great Deep Waters covered the world."
>
> Immediately I foresaw the coming legend, so crept into the shell of monosyllables.
>
> "No?" I questioned.
>
> "No," he replied. "For one time there was no land here at all; everywhere there was just water" (pp. 69-70).

"Crept into the shell of monosyllables" is good; it is very good indeed. She is a marvellous fiction writer.

Visitors Who Never Left

Boas and Barbeau provide a broad foundation for Tsimshian mythography. Frances Robinson, editor of *Visitors Who Never Left* (University of British Columbia Press 1974), refers to them regularly as analogues. It is a way of supplying a sense of tradition, and it works to our benefit. We accept the stories of *Visitors Who Never Left* much more readily than the *Sepass Tales,* even though the process of transmission shows similarities:

> The present collection of myths is the work of Kenneth B. Harris, *Hagbegwatku,* who persuaded his uncle, Arthur McDames, to record them in 1948. They have not been tampered with in any way and are given exactly as translated by Ken Harris, using his own divisions and order. These are his stories, presented exactly as he understands them. . . . These myths were originally taped in *Tsomalia,* described by Ken Harris as the mother tongue of the Gitksan and used by Arthur McDames. Ken's mother, Mrs. Irene Harris, a woman in her

eighties, was one of the few people left who could translate them. Mrs. Harris agreed to translate the stories into his language for Ken who could then put them into English to be written down (pp. xvii-xviii).

Until linguistic specialists listen to the McDames tapes and analyze the glossary of Sepass's "ancient language" provided by Eloise Street, both productions will be suspect. But Frances Robinson shows, as Eloise Street does not, that Ken Harris's versions fit into an ongoing tradition.[14]

The most immediate previous item in the tradition is *Men of Medeek* (Kitimat: Northern Sentinel Press 1962), stories told by Walter Wright and taken down by Will Robinson of Terrace in 1935. In fact, Ken Harris lived with Walter Wright for three years (1936-39) "as part of the Indian way of getting to understand relatives in different areas and of making sure that the myths remain faithful to the original" (p. 22). They listened to each other's versions of the stories, and "it became clear to Ken that Walter Wright's versions were Tsimshian in language and thought, not Gitksan" (p. 22). This distinction is not something that we, at our distance from the materials, can feel. Two of the stories in *Men of Medeek* are basically the same as Harris's stories of the Goat feast and the vengeance of the Medeek (as Frances Robinson points out, pp. 50-51 and 59-60). For the rest, Walter Wright seems to have wanted to tell Will Robinson what amounts to the histories, territories,

---

[14]Frances Robinson is on the staff of the Department of Fine Arts, University of British Columbia. Her son, Michael, was an anthropology student at the time of the book's preparation, and "introduced me," she says (p. xx), "to myth analysis." We should not give the impression that Frances Robinson's scholarly apparatus is very thorough or definitive. See a comparison between *Visitors Who Never Left* and Barbeau's *Downfall of Temlaham* by Elli Köngäs Maranda, "B.C. Indian Myth and Education" *B.C. Studies* No. 25 (Spring 1975) pp. 125-134. For another view of Ken Harris, see Norman Newton's *Fire in the Raven's Nest* (Toronto: New Press 1973) pp. 81-82.

and laws of the Kitselas, and involves a great deal of feuding and unnecessary bloodshed and treachery. Walter Wright in his Preface says that he wanted the record written down so that his scattered people may "come to have an honest pride in their lineage, and in the deeds performed by their ancestors" (p. 2). He will probably fail in this aim; for his powers of narration are not sufficient to make squabbling over territory and massacre for the sake of "honour" seem laudable.[15]

Histories, Territories, and Laws of the Kitwancool is of the same genre, an apologia for the aristocratic families, a series of heraldic glosses:

> The first is the story of the leading Wolf group (W1), of their early home on the sea-coast at the site of the present Prince Rupert, of their travels up the Nass River, and their establishment in their present territory. The second, dealing with the Nee-gamks pole, tells how Gwennue and his people (F3) tried to find their way back to their ancestral home of Dam-la-ham on the Skeena after the flood had carried them west to Alaska, and of their adventures along the way. Next, the story of the Ha-ne-lal-gag pole traces the travels of a band of Interior people from the headwaters of the Skeena (F1), tells how they took possession of much of the the Upper Nass, and finally came to form part of the tribe.[16]

---

[15]This must be the same Walter Wright whom G.B. Gordon of the University of Pennsylvania Museum interviewed in 1917: "Walter lives on the Skeena River between Kitsamkalum and Lakelse in Northern British Columbia. He is well known and respected by the white settlers in that district. He is an industrious Indian and works night and day at his fishing and in the new logging camps or on the ranches to support his family, which includes not only a wife and children but mother-in-law and nephews and nieces to the number of twenty or more"— *The Museum Journal* 9 (March 1918) 39. Gordon published a few stories, very similar to *Men of Medeek,* under the title, "Legends of Kit-selas" (pp. 39-49).

[16]*Histories, Territories, and Laws of the Kitwancool* ed. Wilson

We have come across plenty of these family crest stories before, in Barbeau. This collection is unique in the way it came into being. Wilson Duff and Michael Kew went up to Kitwancool in 1958 to negotiate the removal of some totem poles for preservation in the Provincial Museum. They offered to replace each one with an exact copy carved in Victoria. The Kitwancool chiefs wanted one additional condition: "that their histories, territories, and laws were to be written down, published and made available to the University for teaching purposes" (p. 3). Of course Duff was happy to agree to this. Mrs. Constance Cox was called upon; she had been Barbeau's interpreter in the 1920s. "As the appointed chiefs narrated the stories, Mrs. Cox translated them into English and Mr. McKilvington wrote them down" (p. 5). B.W. McKilvington was a Wolf Clan chief married to the schoolmistress in the village. The manuscript notebook was typed and gone over by Wilson Duff, and resubmitted for further correction. This procedure produced what must be one of the most authentic groups of texts in existence anywhere, from the point of view of Native input.

The erratic and occasionally disjointed quality of the narration confirms how strictly verbatim it is. This is its charm. At the same time, no one could call these stories aesthetic accomplishments. Family crest narratives rarely are; they are heavy with events, but very light on plot. Without a reasonably suspenseful story line, the happenings gain their importance outside the story itself: what transpired is significant because it happened to one's own ancestors. Outsiders cannot be expected to get much pleasure from learning the details of how one is descended from the Chief Frog's sister.

The Bookbuilders of Ksan in their postscript to *We-gyet Wanders On* (Hancock House 1977) make a distinction between history and story:

Tribal histories and laws were taught with stern

Duff (B.C. Provincial Museum, Anthropology in British Columbia Memoir No. 4, 1959) p. 13.

accuracy of detail but the ordinary stories and legends were often colored by the personality of the storyteller. A bloodthirsty person emphasized the cruel and frightening, a gentle, witty person brought out the humor and compassion (p. 73).

In 1971, with a Government grant, the bookbuilders taped all they could get of the old ways and stories, amassing a surprising amount.[17] "We have it in our hearts to build this wealth into several lively and informative publications" (p. 73). They lead off, luckily for us, with the liveliest material, the stories of their trickster-raven, We-gyet.

Ken Harris had one such story, "Weeget and the Water," which is quite similar to their "We-gyet and Water." The only water in the world at that time belonged to a woman, who guarded it carefully. The trick We-gyet used was to chew up some bark into a pulpy, brown mass and insert it under her blanket while she slept. Then he woke her up, and pointed to what he said she had done. She fled out in embarrassment, and he was able to steal the water. As he flew around he spilt it everywhere, thus forming the rivers and lakes of today. There is nothing like this—nor anything so well told—in *Histories, Territories, and Laws of the Kitwancool*.

The Haisla of Kitimat have Weegit stories. Gordon Robinson includes a few lively ones in his *Tales of Kitamaat* (Kitimat: Northern Sentinel Press 1956). Gordon (from his friendly photograph it is clear that we are on a first name basis immediately) was born in Kitamaat village in 1918, attended Coqualeetza School in Sardis, went back home to teach, worked for the Indian Agency in Alert Bay, and then as Personnel Officer for the Aluminum Company of Canada in Kitimat, where he was chief councillor of the village 1950-54. The book is small, but it obviously contains all the stories of

---

[17]It is well known that a non-Native resident of the Ksan community, Polly Sargent, deserves recognition for her contribution to the success of Ksan's numerous enterprises. She apparently prefers not to claim any credit in print, and thus leaves her role unclear.

the area that he remembers at all well. For good measure, he adds an apocryphal "Katsilanoo Meets Captain Vancouver."

An Early Nootka Collection

Alfred Carmichael of Victoria published a pleasant book of *Indian Legends of Vancouver Island* (Toronto: The Musson Book Company 1922) with a refreshingly informative Introduction. He is very precise about how the collection of legends from his local Seshahts (Alberni Nootka) came to be compiled:

> Some thirty years ago when I first knew the Seshahts, they still celebrated the great Lokwana dance or wolf ritual on the occasion of an important potlatch, and I remember well the din made by the blowing of horns, the shaking of rattles, and the beating of sticks on the roof boards of Big Tom's great potlatch house, when the Indians sighted the suppositional wolves on the river bank opposite the Village.
>
> In those days we were permitted to attend the potlatches and witness the animal and other dances, among which were the "Panther," "Red Headed Woodpecker," "Wild Swan" and the "Sawbill Duck." Generally we were welcome at the festivals, provided we did not laugh or show sign of any feeling save that of grave interest. Among my Indian acquaintances of those days was Ka-coop-et, better known in the district as Mr. Bill. Bill is a fine type of Seshaht, quite intelligent and with a fund of humour. Having made friends, he told me in a mixture of broken English and Chinook some of the old folk lore of his tribe. Of these stories I have selected for publication "How Shewish Became a Great Whale Hunter" and "The Finding of the Tsomass." This latter story as I present it, is a composite of three versions of the same tale, as received, by Gilbert Malcolm Sproat about the year 1862; by myself from "Bill" in 1896,

and by Charles A. Cox, Indian Agent, resident at Alberni, from an old Indian called Ka-kay-un, in September 1921....

The framework for "The Legend of Eut-le-ten," was related to me by Rev. M. Swartout in the year 1897. Mr. Swartout was a missionary to the West Coast Indian tribes. He spoke the language of the natives fluently, and took great pains to get the story with as much accuracy as possible. A few years later, Mr. Swartout was drowned during a heavy storm while crossing in an open boat from the islands in Barkley Sound to Ucluelet.

In the making of the stories into English, I have worked in what knowledge I have of the customs and habits of the West Coast Indians of Vancouver Island. In a few instances, due to a lack of refinement of thought in the original stories, I have taken some license in their transcription. The legends indicate the poetry that lies hidden in the folk lore of the British Columbia Coast Indian tribes (pp. 5-6).

I have quoted Carmichael at length because I value his loquaciousness. If only others would take the space he does to say exactly what they are doing. Not much of his small collection is his own—but he doesn't pretend it is. One is quite clear where one stands with him. These are not very competent stories; but, knowing where and how Carmichael got them, I feel that they have, as "found objects," a stronger linkage to traditional Indian history than something created with deliberate artistry, such as, for instance, in the same locality, the books of George Clutesi.

George Clutesi

"This series of Indian folklore tales," George Clutesi writes in his Introduction to *Son of Raven, Son of Deer* (Sidney, B.C.: Gray's Publishing Ltd. 1967), "will endeavour to reach the more sensitive, the more sympathetic and the more reasoning segment of the non-Indians, who may have some willingness

164

to study and understand the culture of the true Indian, whose mind was imaginative, romantic and resourceful" (p. 9). In the dozen stories in this collection, Clutesi, an accomplished Nootka (Tse-shaht) artist, rewrites often-told stories of his tribe. They have had, as he hoped, great success in the white world, where they have stood up quite well as bedtime stories in competition with Hans Christian Andersen. Unfortunately, whatever moves he makes towards white sensibility are taking him further away from what we are here interested in, the traditional oral presentation of legends. Yes, he is "imaginative, romantic and resourceful" as a creative writer. The result borders on fiction, which category has been completely excluded from consideration in this *Guide,* as have, equally, such non-Native fictionalizations as those of Christie Harris, who also claims to be interpreting Indian lore to the white world.[18]

A similar objection applies to Clutesi's *Potlatch* (Sidney, B.C.: Gray's Publishing Ltd. 1969). "This narrative is not meant to be documentary," says the author's preface. "In fact it is meant to evade documents. It is meant for the reader to feel and to say I was there and indeed I saw" (p. 5). *Potlatch* is extremely well-written, but I do not feel I was there. A stark

---

[18]An earlier Christie Harris was Isabel Ecclestone Mackay, a poetess who died just before her *Indian Nights* was published (Toronto: McClelland and Stewart 1930). She got help "in the preparation of these legends" from three local Vancouver men of talent and distinction, Judge Howay, R.L. Reid, and Charles Hill-Tout. The latter writes a Foreword to the tales, in which he is willing to say that, "All ring true and are saturated through and through with the genuine psychology of the Indian" (p. 14). This is praise appropriate to an obituary. Actually, *Indian Nights* has the genuine psychology of a Victorian lady water-colourist.

Just published (from Theytus Books in Nanaimo, 1981) is *Kwulasulwut: Stories from the Coast Salish,* in which Ellen White, a teacher of Native traditions in a local elementary school, presents five tales in the manner she has found successful in the classroom. It is appropriate to mention this book here because the style she adopts is quite similar to that used in most children's books currently.

documentary is exactly what would have accomplished his purpose. It is a paradox that Clutesi offers himself as a doorway into the Native experience and then blocks our entry with works of art.

Copper Woman

Anne Cameron (Cam Hubert), who wrote the screenplay for a successful TV drama involving Vancouver Island Indians ("Dreamspeaker"), has now published a curious book, *Daughters of Copper Woman* (Vancouver: Press Gang 1981), which we must conclude lies within the genre Defoe created with *Moll Flanders,* i.e. fictional works which repeatedly and almost convincingly assert that they are drawn with fidelity from actual experience. She purports to be recounting stories and sayings as told to her by a personage called "Granny" of Ahousat: "The style I have chosen most clearly approaches the style in which the stories were given to me" (p. 7). Though a West Coast Indian woman is named on the first page, it is never categorically stated that she is "Granny."

There would be a lot of new information here if one could believe it, if one could believe, for instance, that the Spaniards forced the Cowichan to work gold mines on Vancouver Island (p. 86). The undoubted power in the book comes from a passionate feminism. It is calculated to annoy anyone who is not a passionate feminist; and I admit that it does annoy me a little to see "The Girl Who Married the Bear" turned into a lesbian story:

> . . . the young woman took the bear's head in her lap, and stroked its fur and kissed its nose, and said "But you're beautiful. Strong, and gentle, and beautiful, and I do love you."
>
> "I'm a female bear," the bear said.
>
> The young woman sat for a long time and then she laughed and said "If I can love a creature that looks as different from me as you do, why should I care if you are a male bear or a female bear? I love you, bear" (p. 118).

"Granny" is something like Castaneda's Don Juan, and probably has the same authenticity.

Teachings of the Tides

David W. Ellis has been listening to West Coast men, particularly Luke Swan of Ahousat and the late Solomon Wilson of Skidegate, in order to satisfy his great curiosity about the marine life of the coastline. *Teachings of the Tides* (Nanaimo: Theytus Books 1981) ends with an interesting chapter on "Supernatural Creatures" of the sea (information from Luke Swan); and *The Knowledge and Usage of Marine Invertebrates by the Skidegate Haida* (Queen Charlotte Islands Museum Society 1981) contains a series of short legends (from Solomon Wilson) pertaining to the subject. Two general legends as told by Solomon Wilson, each with a paragraph of commentary—rare native interpretation—appear in *The Charlottes* Volume 5 (1980), also published by the Museum Society, pp. 4-9. More are to be expected. Ellis's legends gain from being a by-product of serious question and answer sessions on marine life, a topic of great interest to both himself and his informants, and of course to Native storytellers from the beginning of time.

S.J. Ross of the Vancouver Public Aquarium assembled seventeen stories concerning interaction between human and marine life from Swanton, Boas, and others, which constitute, with illustrations, a very tasteful issue of the Aquarium *Newsletter*, vol. 19, no. 6 (November-December 1975).

An older anthology organized by sea, air, and land creatures was William L. Webber's *The Thunderbird "Tootooch" Legends* (Vancouver 1936, revised 1952). This miniature encyclopedia has interest, but the story material has been removed by paraphrase far from any authentic source. "The stories have been collected during the past ten years from various Indian Tillicums, and some have been taken from the works of Boas and Staunton [sic]" (p. 7.).

167

Anthony Carter — "Somewhere Between"

Anthony Carter was with the Royal Canadian Air Force at Sandspit on the Queen Charlotte Islands during the war, and always planned to return. He did so as the consummate photographer of *This is Haida* (1968). His myth-collecting is secondary to the photographs. There is none in the Haida volume; but in *Somewhere Between* (1966) and *Abundant Rivers* (1971) he includes legends he had gathered first hand from the Squamish, Stalo, and other tribes, such as told to him

> one very pleasant afternoon at the house of one of our most interesting and charming oldtimers, Dominic Charlie, a full-blooded Squamish Indian, with a wit and humor to match his very agile 84 years (*Abundant Rivers* p. 26).

There is a loving quality in the colour of the photographs; they are very gentle in their honesty. The stories are the same. As a fish-packer for years along the coast, Anthony Carter came to his Indians from the water, and obviously got the kind of welcome appropriate to that traditional way of making a visit.

Additional Local Collections

Like Anthony Carter, Marjorie Talbot visited the Burrard Reserve and listened to the stories and opinions of Chief George and his wife Ta. She published a detailed report of the experience as *Old Legends and Customs of the British Columbia Coast Indians* (New Westminster, B.C. 1952), which includes a lengthy version of the Great Serpent legend.

Soogwilis (Toronto: Ryerson Press 1951) is "a collection of Kwakiutl Indian designs and legends" compiled by R. Geddes Large, son of Dr. R.W. Large, a medical missionary on the B.C. coast, mainly from one of his father's patients, Charlie George of Fort Rupert. Some motifs are familiar, such as the wife captured by the killer-whale; but the material has all been "woven into one narrative" along the lines of Barbeau's popularizations of the '40s (he is thanked in the Foreword, p. 9). The drawings, "undoubtedly crude" (p. 9), are the more valuable for having been left untouched by the compiler.

Mrs. B.M. Cryer published five "legends of the Cowichans" as *The Flying Canoe* (privately printed, no date, around 1949); but this constitutes only a small fraction of the myriad Cowichan stories and articles she contributed to the columns of the Victoria *Daily Colonist* in the years 1932-36. Mrs. Cryer obviously had fast friends among the Cowichan Indians, and has an engaging personal way of recounting what they told her. However, something in the style suggests severe limitation in her comprehension of what she heard. If her work is ever collected for publication, it should be through the agency of an expert ethnologist in the area.[19]

In the early sixties, the ladies of the Folklore Committee of the B.C. Indian Arts and Welfare Society, did an interesting piece of what they called "verbal archaeology." They conducted an essay contest among the Indian school children on Vancouver Island. In the first year the children mainly wrote about what they had seen on television; but, with persuasion, the essays in later years began to change: "It was obvious that the children were going to their elders for information and that they were being told some of the almost forgotten stories, customs and beliefs—thus the Foreword (p. vi) to the published result, *Tales from the Longhouse* "by Indian Children of British Columbia" (Sidney, B.C. 1973). The Committee "derived great pleasure from the preparation of this book" (p. vii) and it is a very pleasurable book. Obviously, part of their pleasure

---

[19]Who will also take cognizance of Cowichan legends collected by Armourer Sergeant J. Humphreys just before the First World War and apparently published in the regimental journal of the 47th Battalion, Canadian Expeditionary Force (see typescript of proposed volume in B.C. Provincial Archives). I am indebted to the B.C. Indian Language Project for this information, and for copies of Mrs. Cryer's articles.

was in cleaning up the grammar and the essays generally: these are rather flawless compositions. On the other hand, there is a nice authenticity about the subject matter. The chief editor, Agnes Carne Tate, states that "all the original essays are on file and may be consulted" (p. vii). The research here would be to find out who helped the children with their homework; for this is a potentially very useful material for studying the transmission of oral tradition from adults to children.

The Story of the Totem (privately printed in Vancouver, 1924) would be negligible but for the evident fact that the meagre legends have a particular source, Mrs. Jane Cook of Alert Bay, and the man who transmitted them, Ronald Campbell-Johnston, had undoubted sincerity.

Tales the Totems Tell by Hugh Weatherby was published by Macmillan of Canada in 1944; it was reprinted six times, and in its paperback form it can, because of the superior distribution methods of Macmillan, be found on bookstalls today where better collections would never be seen. The stories, wherever they originally came from (it is not indicated), have obviously been re-written drastically. The publisher's blurb, in stating that "Mr. Weatherby presents these stories as they were told to him by the Indians," will not be taken literally.

Margaret Bemister's *Thirty Indian Legends,* originally compiled in 1912, and published by Macmillan of Canada in 1917, is now republished by J.J. Douglas, 1973. The preface asserts that "for the most part the legends here told are drawn from original sources" (p. 3), but we are not made aware of what field work the compiler did. She was based in Winnipeg, and thanks a Mr. Gunn and a Mr. Linklater for two of the stories, and a Mr. Logie of Summerland, B.C., for "The Chief's Bride" (which, however, does not appear by that title in the collection). She also thanks "the Okanagan chief,

Antowyne, for the other Okanagan Legends"; so that presumably those were obtained first hand. All the stories are sparsely written, with an even tone; the way in which she adapts a G.M. Dawson story is indicative of a fairly inoffensive hand.

While editor of *The Ladner Optimist* in 1946-47, Geraldine McGeer Appleby talked to some of the older residents of the Tsawwassen reserve, chiefly Joe Splockton (who was also Norman Lerman's informant soon afterwards), and published a series of a dozen legends in the newspaper. They were collected in 1961 as *Tsawwassen Legends,* published by Dunning Press, Ladner. Geraldine Appleby's style is open and candid in the best newspaper reporting style, so that Joe Splockton's own voice seems to be heard within it. These stories are a valuable addition to the corpus.

A series of equally valuable legends, as yet uncollected, appeared in the *Penticton Herald* in 1936-38, written up by Isabel Christie of Oliver, B.C., from the story-telling of Mrs. Josephine Shuttleworth, as translated by Miss Louise Shuttleworth. Josephine Shuttleworth's father, Francois, was Chief of the Penticton Band at the time of the first European entry into the area (as one of the items narrates). I am indebted to Duane Thomson of Okanagan College, and the B.C. Indian Language Project, for the pleasure of perusing photocopies of the newspaper clippings of these stories, which will be especially significant for anyone following the adventures of Coyote.

B.A. McKelvie, a staff writer for the Vancouver *Province* for many years, was the author of a history of Fort Langley and several other local histories. He published privately in 1941 his *Legends of Stanley Park*. He remarks in the Foreword that "a different legend of Siwash Rock is related than that told by the late Pauline Johnson. The moral is the same, the virtue of unselfishness, but the story itself is less familiar to the public. Yet it was told to me by a Squamish chief as being older and more authentic than the other." He does not name his Squamish source. It is a newspaperman's prerogative not to.

II
Anthologies

The most ambitious "anthology" of Northwest Coast myth and legend is the long section of Boas's *Tsimshian Mythology* (1916) entitled "Comparative Study of Tsimshian Mythology" (pp. 565-881), which categorizes Tsimshian mythology (which is almost, though not quite, coextensive with the mythology of the Northwest Coast as a whole) and deals with sources and analogues. In so doing, it paraphrases in varying degrees of fullness all the gathered narratives published up to that time. Barbeau's two-volume *Totem Poles* (1950) anthologizes, again often in paraphrase, all that he and others had collected of the stories behind the totem poles of the whole of the Northwest Coast. Boas and Barbeau have their own particular scholarly purposes, and do not pretend to fulfill the usual aim of an anthology, which is to present a sample of literary material in a pleasing way. However, these two monumental works provide, as a welcome by-product, a sense of the extent and richness of the oral traditional literature of the area.

Stith Thompson's *Tales of the North American Indians* (Indiana University Press 1929) utilizes quite a number of tales from British Columbia; their prominence in his discussion of myth-motifs is helpful to students who wish to apply that particular scholarly approach. Again, the anthology aspect is subordinate to the analytical intention. We will now turn to a variety of anthologies which have the common goal of presenting myths and legends for general reading or study.

Katharine Berry Judson in the Preface to her *Myths and Legends of British North America* (Chicago 1917) lists the impeccable sources for her legends: Bureau of Ethnology, Jesup Expedition, Memoirs of the Museum of Natural History, and the Canadian Bureau of Mines. [20] From what one can immediately recognize from the West Coast—part of John Sky's version of the Raven cycle, for instance, on pp. 22-24—her precis is severe but honest.

Mabel Burkholder in *Before the White Man Came* (Toronto: McClelland and Stewart 1923) aimed "to collect the most attractive and important legends cherished among the Indians, especially those told in connection with well-known places" (pp. 7-8). So in her "Legends of the Pacific" section, she includes stories of "The Lions" peaks, Capilano Canyon, and Siwash Rock. The stories seem remote from any viable source. There is no indication of where they were obtained.

George H. Griffin in *Legends of the Evergreen Coast* (Vancouver: Clarke and Stuart 1934) rewrites twenty-four legends (from various unacknowledged sources) in order to meet the tastes of his time. The source for "How the Lynx Won the Elk Maiden" is clearly Charles Hill-Tout (*The Salish People* Vol. I pp. 66-73). In that original version Lynx wins the Elk Maiden by getting her pregnant. Not so in Griffin's version, which substitutes a trite romantic elopement.

---

[20]An earlier anthology *Myths and Legends of the Pacific Northwest* [i.e. Washington and Oregon] (Chicago 1910) gained her a rare Boas review, in *Journal of American Folklore* 24 (1911) 254, which is short enough to quote in full:

> This is a miscellaneous collection of Indian tales, chiefly from the Pacific coast, gathered from older collections, and rewritten according to the literary taste of the author. Although the reader is assured that a consistent effort has been made to tell these stories as the Indians told them, the student of folk-lore will go back to the original sources. To the general reader the collection is entertaining, a little cumbersome by being overburdened with badly-spelled Indian names, but entirely misleading so far as they may be intended to give an impression of the true character, scope, and form of Indian mythologies. The book is accompanied by excellent illustrations representing Indian types and Western scenery.

Ella E. Clark did a certain amount of myth collecting of her own in the United States and also incorporated material from manuscript sources for her *Indian Legends of the Pacific Northwest* (1953) and *Indian Legends from the Northern Rockies* (1966), but previously published legends predominate, and in *Indian Legends of Canada* (McClelland and Stewart 1960) almost entirely so. As far as the West coast is concerned, she does not seem to have cast her net very far; for instance, she ignores Swanton on the Haida, and turns to Deans instead, backed up by Hill-Tout and Alice Ravenhill, who are both using other people's material; so that Clark is giving it three times removed. She includes one Nootka story—from George Hunt, ignoring Sapir. The Kwakiutl and Tsimshian are not represented at all. She prefers rather short and easy stories.

Alice Ravenhill's *Folklore of the Far West* (1953), with its good Canadian title (as opposed to the "northwest," which is, of course, the U.S. perspective), contains fifty-two representative legends from the B.C. area. She has used Boas's *Tsimshian Mythology* (1916) to survey the corpus, and has chosen one version of each of the more popular tales. Her rewriting is fresh and inoffensive—insofar as any rewriting can be. The book was published privately (nominally by the B.C. Indians Arts and Welfare Society, of which the author is listed as "founder and president emeritus"), and is no longer in print.

Alice Ravenhill's contribution is remarkable, since it was a labour of her retirement years. She was seventy-eight at the time of her first publication, *The Native Tribes of British Columbia* (1938). She gained recognition from funding agencies, and her other publication, *A Cornerstone of Canadian Culture* (1944) was published as No. 5 of the Occasional Papers of the British Columbia Provincial Museum. This volume includes illustrations of mythical beings and crests, and summaries of the associated myths.

It was still possible, until recently, to compile from local used bookstores a complete set of the British Columbia Heritage

Series, *Our Native Peoples,* published as Social Studies Bulletins by the Department of Education. The ten pamphlets, researched by A.F. Flucke of the Provincial Museum, are:

(1) *Introduction to Our Native Peoples* (1966)
(2) *Coast Salish* (1965)
(3) *Interior Salish* (1966)
(4) *Haida* (1952)
(5) *Nootka* (1966)
(6) *Tsimshian* (1966)
(7) *Kwakiutl* (1966)
(8) *Kootenay* (1952)
(9) *Déné* (1953)
(10) *Bella Coola* (1964).

Since all the descriptions of the tribal areas include a section of legends from the more obvious, reliable sources, anyone who managed to acquire a set of the above also has a modest anthology of stories.

Claude Mélançon's *Indian Legends of Canada* was published first in French in 1967 and translated for Gage Publishing (Toronto) in 1974. Thus, two extra translations intervene between us and the Native text. This really does not matter, however, since the stories (a spot check indicates) have in any case been adapted ruthlessly from their sources in the ethnographic collections.

John S. Morgan's juxtaposition of North American (mainly Canadian) Indian mythological stories with Greek myth in *When the Morning Stars Sang Together* (Book Society of Canada 1974) adds nothing to the corpus, and plays fast and loose with the myths themselves; but it is notable for its basic premise: that our mythographic concerns are no less significant than those of classical scholars.

In a small pamphlet, *Haida Legends* (Intermedia Press 1976), an artist, Tora, presumably non-Indian, has chosen two

Swanton legends to reprint and illustrate. The surprise here is that, in spite of the claim that the legends are now "more accessible," Swanton's text has not been changed very much and the drawings are not at all elucidatory. The publication is valuable only in that the myths are presented as pleasing in themselves; with possibly the further principle, that the more you pay for something the more you will appreciate it.

In *Illustrated Legends of the Northwest Coast Indians* (not dated, but around 1976) Sharon Hitchcock, a Haida carver and painter in the Fine Arts Department of the University of British Columbia, has chosen to retell and illustrate five legends of the coastal tribes. Money was available from the Indian Resources Centre, and the pamphlet was produced with the cooperation of the B.C. Native Indian Teachers' Association.

CommCept Publishing Ltd. of Vancouver, a new house dedicated to getting well-produced up-to-date texts into the public school libraries and classrooms, offers *Indian Tales of the Northwest* (1976), twenty-three pieces from the published corpus, somewhat re-written by Patricia Mason with children in mind. David L. Rozen, as ethnology consultant, adds a brief introduction and bibliography. The stories are chosen to provide an enjoyable reading experience. Perhaps a school-teacher reading these to a young class is as near the original performance situation as we can expect to find at the present time. If the teacher feels the need to say something about these stories, the publisher has provided a *Teacher's Guide* in a separately bound paperback. The hints as to possible teaching activities, such as role playing, field trips, puppet shows, chronological comparison, and cross-cultural comparison, are quite edifying. In this subject we should all go back to elementary school.

Recent Myth-Collecting
by Ethnologists and Linguists

This section would be much larger if we were in a position to discuss a number of important collections still in manuscript. Wayne Suttles is known to have an ample body of Musqueam texts, Bruce Rigsby has Nass Gitksan, Jay Powell has Kwakiutl, and Brent Galloway has Halkomelem, to list only a few of those not mentioned below. A number of scholars have collected short dictated texts for linguistic purposes, the cumulative effect of which will certainly make itself felt in mythography. Lawrence C. Thompson in "The Northwest" section of Thomas Sebeok's *Native Languages of the Americas* (1976) has summarized ongoing scholarship in this very active area of anthropology. Here we can briefly comment, from a non-specialist point of view, on the myth and legend that has come to the surface in published form.[21]

Ronald L. Olson

The categories "free-lancer" and "scholar" are anything but rigid. Much fine scholarship has been exhibited among the "free-lancers," as I hope I have been able to show. When we come to our first academic, Ronald Olson, we see that he has much of the flair we would associate with someone outside the academy. All his ethnographic work was university sponsored, and he was a mainstay of the Department of Anthropology at Berkeley from 1931 to retirement in 1956;

---

[21]As an example of marginally published work, we have the series from the B.C. Indian Advisory Committee Project mimeographed in twenty-nine copies only, mainly for the various tribes involved (the Provincial Museum and the University of British Columbia each have one copy). Susanne Storie recorded the legends in the summer of 1968, and was joined by Jennifer Gould in 1969. The "publications" are dated 1973, and have an introduction by Wilson Duff; they include *Bella Bella Stories, Klemtu Stories, Oweekano Stories,* and *Bella Coola Stories.*

yet his excellence as a field worker was due to a genial, outgoing, non-bookish nature. He was a small-town Minnesota boy, who had also done logging in British Columbia forests for a number of years as a young man. His success as a teacher was also due to this same common touch, according to the fine tribute written by Philip Drucker[22] in the *American Anthropologist* 83 (1981) 605-607:

> He organized a factually good solid course, for its time, but then when he leaned over the lectern, grinning his warm "big Swede" grin, he added something. Some of the rollicking fun of bunkhouse yarns, perhaps. Some of the mystique of Indian traditions. Something loosely called showmanship (p. 606).

This image of him as a "timber-beast" (Drucker's word) helps one to see behind his rather terse and circumspect ethnographic reports.

Olson's three chief reports on B.C. tribes contain myth and legend throughout, mainly origin legends for clans, crests, and dances. They are all published as monographs in the University of California *Anthropological Records* series: (1) *The Social Organization of the Haisla of British Columbia* Vol. 2 (1940) pp. 169-200; (2) *Social Life of the Owikeno Kwakiutl* Vol. 14 (1954) pp. 213-259, including "Miscellaneous Tales" pp. 256-258; (3) *Notes on the Bella Bella Kwakiutl* Vol. 14 (1955) pp. 319-348—note especially "The Life Story of a Bella Bella Woman" pp. 341-343 as showing how much of an individual's progress in his or her society is associated with ritual and hence mythology.[23] The texts were obtained through

---

[22]As for Philip Drucker himself, he presents "Tales of Supernatural Experience" and a few other miscellaneous stories throughout *The Northern and Central Nootkan Tribes* (Bureau of American Ethnology Bulletin 144, 1951). It is difficult to imagine that he has not other myth and legend materials filed away somewhere.

[23]"Related by Mrs. Moses Knight, a member of the Blackfish sept. . . . Mrs. Grant of Kitimat acted as interpreter. Mrs. Knight

interpreters, and sometimes seem to border on precis form. They were intended more to support ethnographic description than to be displayed for any intrinsic beauties, and will therefore have limited use in studying the way oral traditional literature works. Olson's field notes, on file at Berkeley, might be revealing.

Aert H. Kuipers

Aert Kuipers of the University of Leiden came to the Department of Slavonic Studies at the University of British Columbia for the years 1951-54, and extended his linguistic interests by gathering vocabulary and grammar for a full-scale exposition of the Squamish Language. He was unable to obtain texts of any length until, returning to Vancouver in the fall of 1956, he engaged the services of "an exceptionally alert informant," Louis Miranda of the Mission Reserve in North Vancouver. He returned to work with Louis Miranda in 1967 and got further texts, subsequently published in the two volumes, *The Squamish Language* (The Hague: Mouton 1967 & 1969). These texts, though usually shorter than Hill-Tout's similar Squamish tales, are exceedingly valuable in being gathered by a trained linguist from a sympathetic and informed native speaker, and presented interlinearly with impeccable linguistic notes.

Kuipers worked for four summers, 1968-1971, with the Shuswap Indians, and received most of the texts in *The Shuswap Language* (The Hague: Mouton 1974) from Charles Draney of Deadman's Creek Reserve near Kamloops, "who would sit up late at night recording and analyzing stories, and who managed, during his busy day, to drop in ever so often to answer the never-ending questions" (p. 9). Draney tells the "Thunder and Mosquito" story in 1970 (pp. 96-97) almost the same as Teit's informant did in 1895. He tells another Teit

---

was an excellent informant." In the same series, Olson's *Social Structure and Social Life of the Tlingit in Alaska* (Vol. 26 [1967] pp. 1-123) also exemplifies his concern with clan legends.

story, "The Trout Children and their Grandparents" (pp. 123-130), in a version which moves Kuipers to unprecedented praise in calling it "a folktale of surpassing beauty, great psychological depth and considerable religious-historical interest":

> The story opens with a lonely old woman who has lost all her relatives, it ends with an old man—her late husband in the Sky-country—dissolving into fog. In between, the whole of Shuswap—and of human—life unfolds, first in our world, then in the underwater Trout-country, then once again on earth, finally in the Sky-country (the magic number four dividing the story as a whole, as it characterizes many of its details). The joys and apprehensions of the parent, the wishes and hesitations of the bride, the sorrows and adventures of childhood, the energy and transgressions of manhood in the fight for survival—every facet of life is reflected. The way the Trout-children for the first time eye our everyday world as something new and strange is a masterly application of *ostranenie;* the comic relief provided by Coyote in the last act is reminiscent of Shakespeare. The final scene: the grandson groping at the fog into which his grandfather has dissolved, vainly trying to collect the trails that keep extending to the snowy mountains—this scene would make a worthy ending for the opera, ballet or film for which this tale provides such an excellent scenario, and which it deserves no less than does, say, the Novgorod bylina about Sadko (pp. 91-92).

I have quoted Kuipers at length because this is possibly the longest sustained passage of literary criticism in existence on a particular story from our corpus, certainly the most broadly cultured.

The B.C. Indian Language Project[24]

Kuipers's work is addressed to the scholarly world; and the fact that his texts are embedded in a linguistic study tends to remove the storytelling from the milieu which fathered it. Charles Draney told the "Trout-Children" story again in 1974, and it is included in *Shuswap Stories* (1979), edited by Randy Bouchard and Dorothy I.D. Kennedy of the B.C. Indian Language Project; but now without apparatus. Indeed, the editors are very retiring; they refrain altogether from exhibiting their expertise. And by including many photographs of the Native people connected with the volume and of the locations where the stories occurred, they are making sure that the book has the feel of belonging to the Shuswap themselves. This seems all to the good. Although I believe that editorial commentaries, even conspicuous footnotes, enliven a collection of texts and provide a reading experience richer than a bare verbatim record, in a book like *Shuswap Stories* editorial ingenuity would be an intrusion. What *Shuswap Stories* is saying in its straightforward tone and simple format is this: "You have in your hand what a few of us old timers of the Kamloops and Chase bands could come up with when asked. We remember the stories this way, and like them well enough just as they are." When it is put like that, there is little doubt which position seems healthier. Yet I am ambivalent, because I think we are searching for an understanding of Indian myth and legend which is fuller and deeper and more meaningful than the present-day practitioners of the art of storytelling can, on the basis of anything they have been recorded as saying *about* the stories, be credited with. A book that is close to what the storytellers themselves would want is an achievement, a prize. But it is not something that we can be entirely content with. It is not something that educated Indians of the

---

[24]The B.C. Indian Language Project is very active at the time of writing. It is a two-person outfit, based in Victoria, B.C., but not a government agency. It is rather like the back-room research units of wartime, composed of civilians free of any particular Command, getting funding where they can and when they can.

future will be content with.

And yet, again, one is ambivalent, because perhaps it is the essential first stage, to get the living word down while it is miraculously still living, and publish it in a way which is true to itself, to try for the primary experience of the unaccommodated text. With *Lillooet Stories,* published as Vol. VI, No. 1 of *Sound Heritage* (1977), the periodical of the Aural History section of the Provincial Archives of British Columbia, editors Bouchard and Kennedy went to the logical step of making a cassette of the two principal storytellers, Charlie Mack and Baptiste Ritchie, available for purchase with the edition. One can hear these gentlemen as well as see them on the cover. It is *their* publication.

This invisibility of the ethnologist behind his work is an interesting phenomenon. In the case of the B.C. Indian Language Project, they put the Indian in the forefront out of respect for his "power," defined in the old sense of guardian spirit, that which gives him moral force and the ability to be strong in himself. They work with and cherish those—mainly older—residents of the reserves who have this power. The stories they publish, and will publish, have that kind of authenticity.

For example, Louis Miranda, Kuipers's revered informant, went on to work closely with Bouchard and Kennedy, and, in the tradition of other Native ethnologists, learned to transcribe Squamish himself. From 1971 to 1981, he wrote out for the B.C. Indian Language Project some two thousand pages of myths and legends with interlinear translation. Several of these narratives were collected in a North Vancouver schools Squamish Indian Studies kit in 1975, and appeared in a series on the Squamish for the *Province* newspaper (12, 19, 26 September, and 3, 10, 17, 24, 31 October 1978). A three-volume ethnography of the Squamish (with most of the information provided by Louis Miranda) is currently in press with Wilfred Laurier University. Miranda received an honorary degree from Simon Fraser University in June 1981 in his eighty-ninth year, in recognition of his position as the scholar

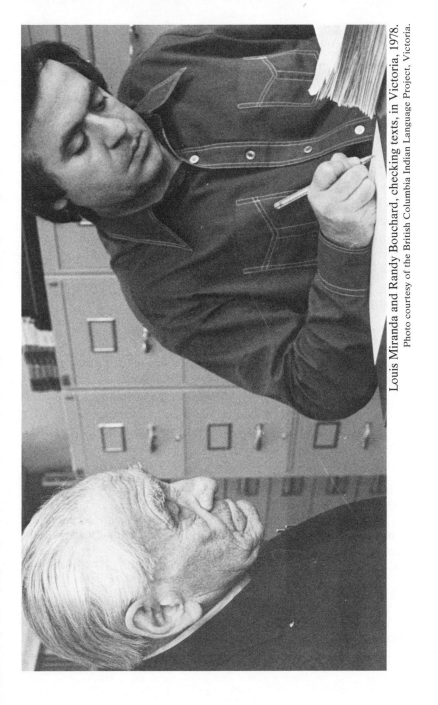

Louis Miranda and Randy Bouchard, checking texts, in Victoria, 1978.
Photo courtesy of the British Columbia Indian Language Project, Victoria.

of Squamish history and language for our time.

The B.C. Indian Language Project is completing two major publishing projects of great interest to the mythographer. *Sliammon Life, Sliammon Land* is the first full scale ethnography of any local tribe in this area since Wilson Duff's *Upper Stalo* of 1953, and includes a healthy number of myths and legends as told in Powell River today. This book is expected from Talonbooks, Vancouver, within a year. The second publication may take a little longer. Columbia University Press has very appropriately accepted the translation of Boas's *Indianische Sagen* which the B.C. Language Project has had in hand for many years. When this opus finally appears, students of myth will no longer have any excuse for not looking at Northwest Coast mythology as a whole, re-evaluating Boas's summaries in *Tsimshian Mythology* (1916), and making some new thoughtful statements about the dominant themes and their significance.[25]

Variations on "Stealing Light"

For his contribution to the Native American Texts Series of the *International Journal of American Linguistics,* Barry F. Carlson, of the University of Victoria, has managed to bring together four texts on the same theme, "Stealing Light."

The Lushootseed text was tape recorded in the early 1950s, from a viable speaker, Harry Moses. Vi Hilbert, a Skagit

---

[25] A selection from *Indianische Sagen* has just appeared with the title "Indian Folktales from British Columbia" in *Malahat Review* for December 1981, pp. 45-77. Dietrich Bertz, the translator, writes a short, informative introduction. The selections are well chosen, and the translation makes pleasant reading. To complete the present picture of the B.C. Indian Language Project's publications in mythology, one should mention "Okanagan Indian Legends," *Okanagan Historical Society 42nd Annual Report* (1978) pp. 10-20. These texts were made available a few years before publication to Pierre Maranda and his co-workers for structural analysis; see Wolfgang G. Jilek and Louise Jilek-Aall "Meletinsky in the Okanagan" in *Soviet Structural Folkloristics* ed. P. Maranda (The Hague: Mouton 1974) pp. 143-149.

Indian and teacher of the Lushootseed language at the University of Washington, collaborated with Thom Hess of the University of Victoria on the transcription of the tape and the language notes.[26] In keeping with the aims of the Series, the presentation of the linguistic aspects of the text overrides any other consideration. There are nine pages of discussion on the Lushootseed language before we get to the text itself. This is presented with an interlinear grammatical word-for-word translation below the original, and then below that is a fairly free translation of each sentence.

This is the general pattern for the other three texts. Thomas Hukari of the University of Victoria collaborated with two graduates of the University's Native language program, Ellen White and Ruby Peter, to produce a similar interlinear text of Ellen White's own version, "Seagull Steals the Sun," in Vancouver Island Halkomelem. Bernice Touchie, also a graduate of that program, recorded her "Stealing Daylight" story from an aged Nitinaht-speaker, Charlie Jones Sr., of Pt. Renfrew. Here the full linguistic analysis is limited to the first four pages, then the rest has a simple word-for-word interlinear translation; and a very much needed free translation is appended.

Robert D. Levine, Assistant Curator of Linguistics at the B.C. Provincial Museum, got his version of the story from Mr. and Mrs. Thomas Hunt of Fort Rupert in 1976-77. There is linguistic analysis and word-for-word translation, with a free translation at the end. Levine, besides being able to capture the interest of a non-specialist reader with his brief sketch of the Kwakwala language, is the only contributor to talk about

---

[26]Another collaboration between Hess and Hilbert appears in *Sound Heritage* Vol. IV Nos. 3 & 4, special issue on "Native Languages and Culture" pp. 39-42. As a sample of "Recording in the Native Language," they present an account the Bone Game, and through careful linguistic analysis reveal the mythological basis for this common pastime. Their work with Leon Metcalf's tape recordings promises to make a major contribution to mythography if they can move from linguistic analysis to myth analysis in this manner.

the circumstances in which the text was obtained. He does not say much, but one comment is particularly interesting:

> The text as given here represents a "composite" of material given by Mr. Hunt and by his wife, Mrs. Emma Hunt. . . . Lines 2-8 represent material supplied by Mrs. Hunt, who described this material as an essential part of the story. It would appear that Mr. Hunt perhaps assumed knowledge of the setting on my part and hence omitted the explanatory material offered by Mrs. Hunt (p. 98).

This is the very briefest beginning of the kind of analysis that mythography, it seems to me, will demand from investigators in the future. Why shouldn't we get to know for certain Mrs. Hunt's intentions in making an interpolation? Why shouldn't we know how we as audience are expected to feel about the Raven at different stages in this story, and what it means when he is described as "the Great Adjuster of the world"? The literal translation at that point is: "adjust going north of northland it's him." Levine must know a great deal more than his average reader in order to convert that literal rendering into "the Great Adjuster of the world," with the full assurance that he is correct. A word from Mr. and Mrs. Hunt on that point would be welcome, and couldn't help but be revealing of the religious meaning they intended the story to have.

Barry Carlson's idea in *Northwest Coast Texts* of getting four expert presentations of the same story in different languages seems an excellent one. He makes no comment on what he thinks can be achieved by studying these texts together. He leaves all that to future mythographers; but he deserves credit for supplying reliable material in a convenient form.

Robin Ridington

Ridington is in the tradition of the great one-tribe anthropologists. He has chosen the Beaver Indians of the Peace River area in the northeast corner of B.C., and he intends to know everything an outsider can know about them. His dissertation, *The Environmental Context of Beaver Indian Behavior* (Harvard University 1968), remains unpublished, as does all his myth material except the stories associated with the prophet dance.[27] Introduced by a detailed description of the cultural context of the prophet dance tradition, they constitute Part 2 of *Swan People: A Study of the Dunne-za Prophet Dance* (National Museum of Man Mercury Series 1978). There is great care in this presentation: care for Charlie Yahey and the other informants, and a slow thoroughness, a self-reflectiveness which makes sure that the ethnologist's stance in relation to the materials does not warp the canvas he is painting.

This is Ridington's methodology:

> Fieldwork was carried out through participant observation during which time extensive use was made of tape recordings of prophetic oratory, songs and stories. These texts were put into English through the use of two tape recorders. The bilingual Dunne-za translator would listen to a passage on the original tape and then record the translation in English on the other machine. These English tapes were then typed out. Minor grammatical revisions were made during this process to reduce ambiguity and improve their flow in writing. The translators reported that often Charlie Yahey used an esoteric vocabulary and referred to people, places, events and concepts they did not fully understand. However, they generally managed to render what he said literally even if they could not explain its entire significance (p. 58).

The authenticity of Ridington's work derives not only from the method of transmission but also from a kinship with

[27]The complete texts of the myths and legends he collected between 1964 and 1968 are deposited in the National Museum of Man (Ottawa), B.C. Provincial Archives, and University of British Columbia Special Collections Library.

Native Indian processes of thought. Linguists have not been very venturesome in translating religious vocabulary. Ridington has. For example, his exposition of the two levels of song among the Beaver is as much "total translation" in its ethnographic depth as Rothenberg's Navajo horse-songs are "total translation" (his phrase) in multi-track tape performance.[28] Rothenberg and Ridington, with the mind-expansion experiences of the sixties behind them, have, each in his own way, got close to the mystical meaning of Indian words. How to let dream give us meaning is something the white American is having to re-learn both from psychology and from races which have never lost the sense that the night has messages as significant as our daytime thoughts. For Ridington, the word "stoned" in its hippie ("tribal") sense is useful as a translation for a kind of medicine-power experience:

> I cannot tell you what "really happens" to children in the bush, just as they cannot tell other people their experience directly. I was told that if a child has the right thoughts, if his head is in the right place, a medicine animal will come to him. There is a moment of meeting and transformation when he

---

[28]Jerome Rothenberg "Total Translation" *Stony Brook* 3/4 (1969) 292-307. To try to attain the "actual indeterminacy of performance," Rothenberg made a recording of his translation of the Twelfth Horse-Song of Frank Mitchell on four tracks, which were then mixed into one. Track 1: "A clean recording of the lead voice." Track 2: "A voice responsive to the first but showing less word distortion and occasional free departures from the text." Track 3: "A voice limited to pure-sound improvisations on the meaningless elements in the text." Track 4: "A voice similar to that on the second track but distorted by means of a violin amplifier . . . a barely audible background filler for the others" (p. 300). The record itself was an insert in *Alcheringa* #2, Summer 1971. Ethnology might be thought of as providing meaning for a text in layers of relative interdeterminacy, something along this model.

is "just like drunk" or in vocabulary more familiar to us, "stoned."[29]

Ridington adds that in these moments the Indian can understand the animal's speech; thus implying that, at depth, translation will have to draw on all the modern research into how animals communicate. Ridington's pushing at the previous limits of translation should soon be providing some interesting experimental publications.

[29]Robin Ridington "Beaver Dreaming and Singing" in *Pilot Not Commander,* ed. Lotz (1971), which is *Anthropologica* 13 (1971) 115-128; quotation on p. 121. See also his article, with Tonia Ridington, "The Inner Eye of Shamanism and Totemism" *History of Religions* 10 (August 1970), reprinted in *Teachings from the American Earth* ed. Tedlock (1975) pp. 190-204, where he states that the children on a vision quest "become, in effect, practicing ethologists, able to understand the behaviour and communications of animals" (p. 199).

Chapter IX
Postscript

Behind all the judgments about authenticity in this book are a number of questions. What is the process of transmission? How did the story get on to the printed page? Are there any field notes or diaries that might reveal how scrupulous the ethnologist was in his procedures? How long was he at the job? How well did he know the language? Did he have a good ear for phonetic dictation? Was it before or after the advent of the tape recorder? Was the story gathered in a performance situation, or with at least one other person present as an audience? Did the informant have status as a storyteller among his people or was it an average member of the tribe trying to remember forgotten things for an honorarium? Is there dramatic subtlety, or too much summary? What is the relation of the English translation to the Native text and literal translation, if such is available? Is the story interesting in its movements and details? Is there internal evidence that it was told with skill and listened to with attention? Does it move us? Does the ethnologist supply a context of tribal information so that we can understand a story to the fullest? Are myth-motifs discussed? Are we given the perspective of a world of archetypes and themes?

These are some of the questions that we have a right to ask when we pull from the shelves an old ethnological collection of tales or a new anthology. The questions will not be answered most of the time. It has not usually occurred to editors that we might be interested in such things. Even where there is authenticity, we are usually expected to take it on faith.

Two volumes worthy of note have been published since the previous chapters were written, one "free-lance," the other "scholarly." We can use them as test cases, and see how they stand up to our questioning.

Kwakiutl Legends "as told to Pamela Whitaker by Chief James Wallas" (North Vancouver: Hancock House 1981) is a volume of about fifty stories—short narratives, large print.

Question 1: What is the process of transmission? It is only from the book's jacket that we learn anything about the collector of these legends, the brief statement: "Pamela Whitaker, a freelance writer, spent three years recording and researching Mr. Wallas' stories." There is no indication of how they were recorded. The appendix gives "a list of the *kwakwala* words which appear in the stories" (p. 204); so one presumes that at one stage James Wallas rendered them in the Native language. But, since Peter J. Wilson, who is described simply as "linguist," is credited with compiling the appendix, we can presume that Pamela Whitaker had no part in translating from the original. Wilson is given no credit as translator; so it must have been James Wallas himself. "James Wallas tells you these stories" (p. 13). If Pamela Whitaker did not revise these English versions for publication, then her role would appear to be limited to bringing the manuscript from Campbell River to North Vancouver. The legends "are as Wallas learned them from his forefathers" (p. 13).

Question 2: What do we know about the storyteller? Peter J. Wilson writes an informative Introduction. James Wallas was born at what is now Port Hardy in 1907.

> At about six to eight years of age, Wallas started
> learning the stories, mostly from his father's eldest

brother. "He knew I was interested and used to invite me over to his fire for tea," he said. "There were not many in the tribe who were interested enough to learn the legends" (p. 9).

He had an active life, trapping, hunting, logging, and fishing. He completed an Indian Education Teachers' Training program in Campbell River and presently "teaches Indian Studies at the Coal Harbour elementary school" (p. 11). Presumably it was his role as a teacher which brought his storytelling to the notice of Pamela Whitaker. He is given the title "Chief," but we are told nothing about his status within his Indian community or any reputation he may have had as a storyteller.

Question 3: Are the stories interesting in themselves? They are quite lively.

> "Do you think you know how to use this canoe?" he asked.
>
> "I'd sure like to try," answered the eighteen-year-old girl.
>
> "Come on in then," said the whale and opened his big mouth. The girl went through his mouth and into his body. He showed her the interior of his tail and fins and how to use them. He took her for a ride in the water.
>
> "This is fun," cried the girl as they skimmed across the waves and down through the deep water.
>
> When they came back to shore the whale said, "How about your sisters? Would they like a ride?" (pp. 148-149)

It is rare to find such exuberance in the Northwest stories as written down. I feel that the above corresponds to the traditional performance of the incident, and James Wallas is using his command of English narrative techniques to portray events with the feeling that he felt when he heard them as a boy. This produces a written text much different from what would have been obtained by an early ethnologist from the same source;

but in some sense it is more authentic, because it gets onto the page the feeling present in storytelling.

Most of these Kwakiutl legends are what we must call "collapsed" versions.[1] The above story is a case in point: traditional tellings would involve an elaborate search for the girl who is taken off by the Killer Whale. Boas lays out the analogues on pp. 840-845 of *Tsimshian Mythology,* where is summarized a great deal of incident involved in the girl's rescue from the land under the sea. James Wallas's story is only a few hundred words long—most of it dialogue; and it ends very simply and surprisingly:

> When the father heard what had happened, he took his canoe and searched out on the water. He looked for many days for his daughter but could not find her.
>
> One day after he had given up the search, one of his younger daughters was walking on the beach. Her lost sister swam up to her and said, "Go and tell my parents I am married now to the killer whale." She was never seen again (pp. 149-150).

There are two things to say about this unusual ending. One is that it does have analogues in a number of stories where human and animal marry and live happily ever after. But even if it didn't, we still have to abide with the fact that this particular performer, James Wallas, wanted the ending as he has it. It works well in its own terms. In fact, in telling these fragments of stories as well as he does, Wallas is, as it were, creating a new genre of well-told fragments. It has happened hundreds of times before that what we know as part of a

---

[1] The useful word "collapsed" for a short tale that we have many longer versions of is coined by Barre Toelken in footnote 7 of the original article, "The 'Pretty Language' of Yellowman" in *Genre* 2 (1969). This piece has now been thoroughly rewritten (with Tacheeni Scott) for *Traditional Literatures of the American Indian* ed. Karl Kroeber (University of Nebraska 1981) pp. 65-116, quoted word on p. 112.

longer cycle is presented as a separate tale; but in *Kwakiutl Legends* we have a whole book full of "bits" from a storyteller of some authority. It is a marker for the way the oral tradition is probably moving in our own time.

Question 4: What kind of ethnographic and mythographic context is provided to help us with the social and thematic significance of the stories? The answer in this case is none at all, beyond the few remarks of Peter Wilson, which pertain to the author and his tribe and not to the legends themselves. The photographs and impressionistic chapter-dividers are nothing more than decorative, and this applies too to prayers interspersed throughout the book. These are from Boas's *The Religion of the Kwakiutl* (1930). Their relevance is not established; and the injecting of this older, ritualistic, devotional voice has a somewhat deleterious effect on the upbeat mood created by James Wallas in his short snappy stories.

Summary: Kwakiutl Legends gets points for Question 3—the stories have their own distinctive value as stories; but the volume fails badly on the other questions, since there is little besides the stories themselves to demonstrate their authenticity or to reveal their value and significance.

Bella Coola Texts by Philip W. Davis (Rice University) and Ross Saunders (Simon Fraser University) is published by the B.C. Provincial Museum as Heritage Record No. 10 (1980). It comprises eighteen texts in Bella Coola, with an interlinear grammatical analysis, a phrase by phrase translation, and a free translation for each.

Question 1: What is the process of transmission? The Introduction merely mentions that the texts were "all recorded in January 1967":

> With the exception of one text, these were related by Mrs. Agnes Edgar, who is a fluent speaker of Bella Coola, then in her mid-seventies. The lone text not related by Mrs. Edgar is Text 16, told by Mr. Dan Nelson, then in his late sixties and also a fluent speaker of the language (p. 3).

There is no comment on the circumstances in which the recordings were made. The texts were obviously tape recorded, and listened to many times—the way the texts are presented reveals that. It is quite clear that we are in the hands of linguistic experts; their previous articles on Bella Coola grammar are listed in the Bibliography. There is a Foreword by Barbara Efrat, Curator of Linguistics at the B.C. Provincial Museum. The work was done with financial backing from the National Science Foundation and the Canada Council; and the scholarly reviews will no doubt confirm the reliability of the linguistic analysis, notes, and glossary. The non-specialist gets a definite impression of competence. The precision is felt too in the phrase-by-phrase translations; one is perfectly convinced that the English is a good counterpart to what is being said in Bella Coola. The free translations are also excellent. In short, the authenticity of the transmission is attested to by the reputation of persons associated with the *Bella Coola Texts* and by the obvious skill and care with which the text and interlinear matter are presented.

Question 2: What do we know about the storytellers? Nothing more than their name and age and the fact that they are fluent speakers of Bella Coola. There is no indication of their attainments, idiosyncrasies, or status in the tribe.

Question 3: Are the stories interesting in themselves? There is a very great range in length and quality in Mrs. Edgar's repertoire, but every story is interesting in the way it is told. At last—almost, it seems, for the first time in the whole corpus of the literature we have been surveying—we can hear the fits and starts, the turns of phrasing, and the play of mind which make up the distinctive idiom of an individual storyteller at work. The interest is in the precise way in which Mrs. Edgar proceeds from point to point and round about in her narrative. The interlinear translation is the really absorbing way to follow her. For instance, Raven has just tricked his female relatives into running ashore from imaginary enemies, while he eats all the berries they have gathered:

The raven began to rub his stomach with what was left over of the berries he had eaten. He rubbed his stomach. It was as if his stomach was bleeding then. They appeared then. They kept on coming. He was stretched out on the bottom of the boat. They started crying right off then. They were mourning him. "Cousin's blood isn't usually this color," they were saying. They cried as they mourned the deceased. This is the way they sang. They sang as they cried while mourning Raven. "This isn't the uusual coolor of Cousin's bloood," they were saying. He suddenly made a rumbling sound in his throat. "Yeess," he said. "It has to be like that when you're in a war," he said all right (pp. 168-170).[2]

The editors have been helpful in letting us hear Mrs. Edgar's funny intonation in places. It would not have hurt to have taken a page out of Dennis Tedlock's *Finding the Center,* and given us more of the rise and fall of pitch and volume and velocity. But such is the fidelity here that we can almost do the musical notation for ourselves, and—following Barre Toelken's "Yellowman"—imagine the places where, in per-

---

[2]The free translation renders this passage:

Raven began to rub his stomach with the leftover berries, and it looked as if his stomach was bleeding. They appeared, saw his bleeding stomach and right off started crying. They mourned him. They cried as they mourned him. They sang as they cried, mourning Raven.

"This isn't the usual colour of Cousin Raven's blood," they said.

Suddenly Raven made a mumbling, gurgling sound in his throat. "Yeess," he said. "War is like that" (pp. 171-172).

Excellent as the free translations usually are, they would not by themselves—and the above is a good example—do justice to Mrs. Edgar's wry modulations. (Since the above was written, Ross Saunders has communicated to me that, while he is responsible for the free translations, the interlinear translation was produced as a concensus among the Bella Coola informants themselves.)

formance, there would be suppressed and open laughter.

When we also discover that Dan Nelson's idiom in Text 16 "A Rescue" is quite different from Mrs. Edgar's, we are happy to realize that we have before us texts which will adequately serve as a basis for a discussion of style.

Question 4: What kind of ethnographic and mythographic context is provided to help us with the social and thematic significance of the stories? Very little; but the editors' Introduction makes two points: (1) There are three genres represented in these stories, the family origin story, the mythic animal story, and the historical narrative. Knowing a story's genre helps us to read it in the proper way. (2) Some stories are also in Boas's *The Mythology of the Bella Coola* (1898) and McIlwraith's *The Bella Coola Indians* (1948). The editors, however, did not consider it appropriate to make any comment on the variants between the versions.

Summary: Bella Coola Texts makes little attempt to woo the reader; it simply presents the texts with such expertise that we need nothing more to convince us of their value to future studies of style and mythography, though certainly more commentary would be welcome.

G.P. Murdock's *Ethnographic Bibliography of North America* 4th edition (1975) Vol. 3 is the place to go for a complete listing of the materials on myth and legend in this area. But it is certainly no guide—one is immediately overfaced by the number of references. Standing in the library before the rows of green-bound Bureau of American Ethnology bulletins and the black-bound reprints of the Jesup Expedition and the brown-bound American Folklore Society series, one is paralyzed. The present *Guide to B.C. Indian Myth and Legend* has tried to sort things out, using criteria based on the methods of myth-collecting, so that the general reader might have some idea where to begin.

The following choice of ten publications is not necessarily a list of those myths and legends which will ultimately prove most rewarding for mythographic study—*Bella Coola Texts* would be high on such a list—but rather the places where I personally would begin in hope of finding some of the pleasure which this oral traditional literature has provided its performers and hearers from time immemorial.

(1) "The Career of a Medicine-Man According to Isaac Tens, a Gitksan" in Marius Barbeau, *Medicine Men on the North Pacific Coast* (Ottawa: National Museum of Canada 1958) pp. 39-54. There is a matter-of-fact quality about this autobiography of Isaac Tens, his successes and failures as a shaman, which is very touching. One is entirely convinced that his "Swanassu Songs" were efficacious, and that their power lies in their imagery.

(2) "The Winter Ceremonial at Fort Rupert, 1895-96" in *The Social Organization and the Secret Societies of the Kwakiutl Indians* by Franz Boas, "Based on Personal Observations and on Notes Made by Mr. George Hunt" (Washington, D.C. 1897) pp. 544-606. This is a speech-by-speech account of how myth and legend is used in important social transactions.

(3) "How the Animals and Birds Got Their Names" and "Beaver and Frog" told by Charlie Mack, with Baptiste Ritchie and Sam Mitchell as audience, are available on cassette with *Lillooet Stories,* eds. Randy Bouchard and Dorothy I.D. Kennedy, published as Vol. VI, No. 1 of *Sound Heritage* (Victoria, B.C.: Provincial Archives 1977). These performed stories have the healthy effect of making one quite dissatisfied with the printed page.

(4) The complete repertoire of Chief Mischelle of Lytton, as told to Charles Hill-Tout, constitutes pp. 21-129 of Vol. I of *The Salish People: The Local Contribution of Charles Hill-Tout* (Vancouver, B.C.: Talonbooks 1978). This is the only place, I think, where a born storyteller is given a broad enough canvas for us to see what an asset such a person would be to a community, a magnificent resource for entertainment and moral worth.

(5) *Traditions of the Thompson River Indians of British*

Columbia (American Folklore Society 1898) was Teit's first book; the care it exhibits in text and footnotes (and in Boas's introduction too) makes it a very fine collection for study.

(6) The ethnological support Teit gave to his myths and legends is matched only by John R. Swanton on the Haida. One could begin with "He who hunted birds in his father's village," in *Haida Texts and Myths* (Washington, D.C.: Bureau of American Ethnology Bulletin 29, 1905) pp. 264-268, and take advantage of Gary Snyder's book-length study of that story.

(7) Probably the best place of all to begin is with the story that has been offered to us as "a masterpiece of Indian oral tradition," *The Girl Who Married the Bear* (Ottawa: National Museum of Man 1970), especially Maria Johns' version on pp. 28-33. Catherine McClellan's introduction explains why.

(8) Attempts to popularize Indian myth and legend have rarely succeeded. Perhaps the most successful is Betty Keller's redaction of Norman Lerman's Stalo collection, *Legends of the River People* (Vancouver: November House 1976), which presents the tales as if told to children around the evening fire.

(9) A promising sign on the horizon is *We-gyet Wanders On* (Saanichton, B.C.: Hancock House 1977), a well-produced bilingual collection, the first of a proposed series to come out of the contemporary taped interviews of the Ksan Book Builders group. There is a mischievous tone to these trickster stories which makes them genuinely amusing.

(10) The only interesting anthology of B.C. Indian myth and legend since Alice Ravenhill's *Folklore of the Far West* (1953) is *Indian Tales of the Northwest* (Vancouver: CommCept Publishing Ltd. 1976). Twenty-three traditional stories from the area have been chosen for school use—quite rightly; for the classroom seems to be the one place where this oral literature will get a proper performance for some time to come.

Table of Field-Trips within B.C. and Resulting Publications

Geraldine McGeer Appleby

Tsawwassen, 1946-47	*Tsawwassen Legends* (1961)

Marius Barbeau (1883-1969)

Port Simpson, December 1914 to February 1915	*Totem Poles* (1950)
Skeena, August 1920, January 1921, summers 1923, 1924, and 1926	*Totem Poles of the Gitksan, Upper Skeena River* (1929) "Tsimshian Songs" in *The Tsimshian: Their Arts and Music* (1951) *Medicine Men on the North Pacific Coast* (1958) *The Downfall of Temlaham* (1928)
Nass River, July-September 1927 and May-October 1929	"Tsimshian Songs" (1951) *Totem Poles* (1950)
Queen Charlotte Islands, summer 1939	*Totem Poles* (1950) *Haida Myths Illustrated in Argillite Carvings* (1953)
Queen Charlotte Islands, Fort Rupert, and Alert Bay, May-September 1947	*Totem Poles* (1950) *Haida Myths Illustrated in Argillite Carvings* (1953)
William Beynon, present as co-worker on practically all the above trips, later sent texts to Barbeau by mail.	*Tsimsyan Myths* (1961)

Franz Boas (1858-1942)

1886

18 September to 3 October, Victoria	*Indianische Sagen* (1895) "Salishan Texts" (1895)
4 October to 26 October, Nawitti and Alert Bay	*Indianische Sagen* (1895) "On Certain Songs and Dances of the Kwakiutl" (1888)
4 November to 10 December, Cowichan, Comox, Nanaimo	*Indianische Sagen* (1895) "Myths and Legends of the Catlotq" (1888) "Notes on the Snanaimuq" (1889)
14-15 December, Vancouver	*Indianische Sagen* (1895)

1888

31 May to 2 June, Vancouver	*Indianische Sagen* (1895)
3 June to 15 June, Victoria	*Indianische Sagen* (1895)
15-30 June, Port Essington	*Indianische Sagen* (1895)
12-15 July, Lytton	*Indianische Sagen* (1895)
15-24 July, Golden and Windemere	*Folk-Tales of Salishan and Sahaptin Tribes* (1917) *Kutenai Tales* (1918)

1889

18-30 July, Victoria	*Indianische Sagen* (1895)
2-12 August, Alberni	*Indianische Sagen* (1895)
25 August to 4 September, Alert Bay	*Indianische Sagen* (1895)
6-14 September, Kamloops	*Indianische Sagen* (1895)

1890

31 July to 10 August, New Westminster	*Indianische Sagen* (1895)
11-21 August, Ladner	*Indianische Sagen* (1895)

British Columbia Indian Language Project (Randy Bouchard and Dorothy I.D. Kennedy)

Okanagan area, visits chiefly 1966-1969

"Okanagan Indian Legends" (1978)

Mount Currie and Lillooet area, visits chiefly between August 1968 and January 1973

Lillooet Stories (1977)

Kamloops and Chase area, visits chiefly 1971-1975

Shuswap Stories (1979)

Powell River, visits 1971-1981

Sliammon Life, Sliammon Lands (projected 1983)

Alexander Francis Chamberlain (1865-1914)

Kootenays, summer 1981

Kutenai Tales (1918)

Edward Curtis (1868-1952)

Vancouver Island & Queen Charlottes, visits during 1910-1914

The North American Indian Vol. 9 (1913) Salish Vol. 10 (1915) Kwakiutl Vol. 11 (1916) Nootka & Haida

Philip W. Davis & Ross Saunders

Bella Coola, visits 1966-67 and later

Bella Coola Texts (1980)

George M. Dawson (1849-1901)

Queen Charlottes, 1878-79

"On the Haida Indians" (1880)

Vancouver Island and adjacent coast, Summer 1885

"Notes and Observations on the Kwakiool People" (1887)

Kamloops area, 1887

"Notes on the Shuswap" (1891)

Frances Densmore (1867-1957)

Neah Bay, Washington, summers of 1923 and 1926

Nootka and Quileute Music (1939)

Chilliwack, September 1926

Music of the Indians of British Columbia (1943)

Wilson Duff (1925-1976)

Fraser Valley, summers 1949 and 1950

The Upper Stalo Indians (1952)

Kitwancool, spring 1958

Histories, Territories, and Laws of the Kitwancool (1959)

Livington Farrand (1867-1939)

Jesup Expedition, 1897

Traditions of the Chilcotin Indians (1900)
"Myths of the Bellabella" in Boas *Tsimshian Mythology* (1969)

Ida Halpern

Cape Mudge, visits 1947-1953 (Billy Assu) Vancouver (with Mungo Martin in 1950s; Tom Willie 1977-80)

Indian Music of the Pacific Northwest Coast (Folkways record 1967)
Kwakiutl (Folkways record 1982)

Port Alberni, visits 1965-72

Nootka (Folkways record 1974)

Charles Hill-Tout (1858-1944)

Resident in Vancouver from 1891; ethnographic field work in lower mainland & Vancouver Island, 1895-1906

The Salish People (1978) gathered his eight full-scale ethnographic reports into four volumes:
Vol. I Thompson (1899) and Okanagan (1911)
Vol. II Squamish (1900) and Lillooet (1905)
Vol. III Mainland Halkomelem (1902) and Chehalis/Scowlitz (1904)
Vol. IV Sechelt (1904) and Southeastern tribes of Vancouver Island (1907)

Diamond Jenness (1886-1969)

McLeod Lake and Fort Graham, summer 1924

The Sekani Indians of British Columbia (1937)
"Sekani Tales" in *The Corn Goddess* (1956)

Hazelton and Fraser Lake area, winter 1924-25

"Myths of the Carrier Indians of British Columbia" (1943)
The Carrier Indians of the Bulkley River (1943)
"Carrier Tales" in *The Corn Goddess* (1956)

Vancouver Island and Fraser Valley, winter 1935-36

The Faith of a Coast Salish Indian (1955)
"Coast Salish Tales" in *The Corn Goddess* (1956)

Aert H. Kuipers

Vancouver, 1951-54, Fall
1956

*The Squamish Language
— 1* (1967)

Vancouver, summer 1967

*The Squamish Language
— 2* (1969)

Kamloops area, summers
1968-1971

The Shuswap Language
(1974)

Norman Lerman (1926-1975)

Chilliwack and Lower
Fraser area, summer 1950

Once Upon an Indian Tale
(1968)
*Legends of the River
People* (1976)

T.F. McIlwraith (1899-1964)

Bella Colla, March-August
1922, September 1923-
February 1924

The Bella Coola Indians

(1948)

Ronald L. Olson (1895-1979)

Kitimat & Rivers Inlet,
1935

*The Social Organization of
the Haisla* (1940)
*Notes on the Bella Bella
Kwakiutl* (1955)

Rivers Inlet, 1949

*The Social Life of the
Owikeno Kwakiutl* (1954)
*Notes on the Bella Bella
Kwakiutl* (1955)

Robin Ridington

Fort St. John area, 1964-71

*Swan People: A Study of
the Dunne-za Prophet
Dance* (1978)

Edward Sapir (1884-1939)

Alberni, September-Decem-
ber 1910 and October
1913-January 1914

Nootka Texts (1939)
Songs of the Nootka Indians
(1955)

John R. Swanton (1873-1958)

Queen Charlotte Islands, September 1900-August 1901

Contributions to the Ethnology of the Haida (1905), "Kaigani Series"
Haida Texts and Myths (1905)
Haida Texts—Masset Dialect (1908)
Haida Songs (1912)

James Teit (1864-1922)

Began ethnographic work September 1894 in and around Spences Bridge

Traditions of the Thompson River Indians of British Columbia (1898)
Mythology of the Thompson Indians (1912)
"European Tales from the Upper Thompson Indians" (1916)
Folk-Tales of Salishan and Sahaptin Tribes (1917)
"Story of Bear" (1926)
"More Thompson Tales" (1937)

Lillooet, 1899-1903

"Traditions of the Lillooet of British Columbia" (1912)

Fraser River Shuswap, 1900 1903 North Thompson Shuswap

The Shuswap (1909)

Inland from Juneau, Alaska, 1903

"Two Tahltan Traditions" (1909)

Okanagan, 1907-1917 Hope, 1913

Folk-Tales of Salishan and Sahaptin Tribes (1917)

Stikine River, 1912 and 1915

"Kaska Tales" (1917)
"Tahltan Tales" (1919)

Oliver Wells (1907-1970)

Chilliwack area, 1962-1966

Myths and Legends of the Staw-loh Indians (1970)

North Vancouver, August & November 1965

Squamish Legends (1966)

Index

214

215

217